"What did my father

Sarah rose and picked up
"It doesn't matter."

"If he's upset you—"

"Logan, I'm not upset." It was true. She was pretty much over Max and his issues with her as a potential bride for his oldest son.

She *wasn't* a potential bride—not for Logan or anyone. And Max had done her no harm.

In fact, their little chat had been a good thing. It had served to remind her that she was single and planned on staying that way. She liked Logan— maybe too much. He was kind and so generous. He made her laugh and she loved being with him. And whenever he kissed her, she wanted him to kiss her again, to keep kissing her and touching her and doing all those wonderful things to her that made her feel desired and satisfied in all the best ways.

But he wouldn't break her heart. She wouldn't let him. What they had together was no lifetime commitment. She wasn't counting on anything. They were both having a wonderful time for as long as it lasted.

And, she promised herself, she was perfectly happy with that.

* * *

MONTANA MAVERICKS:
Six Brides for Six Brothers

Dear Reader,

Welcome back to Rust Creek Falls, Montana, where rapscallion rancher Maximilian Crawford is determined to find brides for his six hot and handsome single sons.

Max's oldest son, Logan, likes pretty women and the single life. Logan never plans to marry.

As for overworked accountant and single mom Sarah Turner, well, let's just say that romance is not on her agenda. The last thing she needs is a man.

But then Logan meets Sarah. The attraction is immediate and powerful. He wants her. A lot. He even finds himself entranced by her adorable five-month-old daughter, Sophia, who seems to return his affection. And no, Logan has no plans to put a ring on Sarah's finger or to be a daddy to her baby.

But for as long as it lasts, he's set on being the best thing that ever happened to Sarah and little Sophia.

Too bad Sarah has sworn off men indefinitely and has zero interest in saying yes to even a single date with Logan—forget about a whirlwind romance.

Logan is very determined, though. And Sarah may not want to admit it, but she is every bit as attracted to him as i.e is to her. And he's so good with her baby, so charming, so generous...

I had such a great time writing this story of two strong-willed, independent people drawn together in spite of their mutual determination to remain steadfastly single. I so hope you enjoy watching Logan and Sarah find love and forever together against all the odds.

All my best,

Christine Rimmer

Her Favorite Maverick

Christine Rimmer

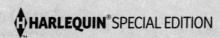
HARLEQUIN® SPECIAL EDITION

Special thanks and acknowledgment are given to Christine Rimmer for her contribution to the Montana Mavericks: Six Brides for Six Brothers continuity.

Recycling programs
for this product may
not exist in your area.

ISBN-13: 978-1-335-57394-0

Her Favorite Maverick

Copyright © 2019 by Harlequin Books S.A.

Printed in U.S.A.

Christine Rimmer came to her profession the long way around. She tried everything from acting to teaching to telephone sales. Now she's finally found work that suits her perfectly. She insists she never had a problem keeping a job—she was merely gaining "life experience" for her future as a novelist. Christine lives with her family in Oregon. Visit her at christinerimmer.com.

Books by Christine Rimmer

Harlequin Special Edition

The Bravos of Valentine Bay

The Nanny's Double Trouble
Almost a Bravo
Same Time, Next Christmas
Switched at Birth

The Bravos of Justice Creek

Carter Bravo's Christmas Bride
James Bravo's Shotgun Bride
Ms. Bravo and the Boss
A Bravo for Christmas
The Lawman's Convenient Bride
Garrett Bravo's Runaway Bride
Married Till Christmas

Montana Mavericks: The Lonelyhearts Ranch

A Maverick to (Re)Marry

Montana Mavericks: The Great Family Roundup

The Maverick Fakes a Bride!

Visit the Author Profile page
at Harlequin.com for more titles.

Thanks to the brilliant and beautiful
Kimberly Fletcher, who named the sweet white
kitten in this story. Kimberly suggested I call the
kitten Opal—and I did. I love that name so much!
As a thank-you, I offered to dedicate this book
to Kimberly. She asked instead that I give her a
different kind of dedication...

Her Favorite Maverick is dedicated to Wildflower
and Miss Clack and to everyone who has survived
cancer. Kimberly would also like to dedicate this
story to those who live with a cancer survivor and to
anyone who has suffered the loss of a loved one to
cancer.

Cancer touches all of us in one way or another.
Fight hard, reach out to those you love and know
that you are not alone.

Chapter One

As Sarah Turner emerged from the tiny back-room office of the former train depot, Vivienne Shuster Dalton glanced up from a worktable covered in fabric swatches, to-do lists, project folders and open sample books.

"There you are," said Viv.

"Just giving it all one more look." Sarah tried for a light tone, but going over the books yet another time hadn't changed a thing. The news was not good.

"Please tell us you've found a solution to our problem."

If only.

Viv's business partner, Caroline Ruth Clifton, stood across the worktable from her. Caroline turned her big dark eyes on Sarah and asked hopefully, "We can swing it, right?"

The answer was no.

And for Sarah, whether she was trying to claw her way up the food chain at the biggest accounting firm in Chicago or working in her dad's little office right here in Rust Creek Falls, Montana, her least favorite part of the job remained the same. She hated telling clients that they were in trouble—especially clients she liked and admired.

Viv and Caroline were a couple of dynamos. They'd even opened a second location down in Thunder Canyon, Montana. Caroline spent most of her time there.

And here in Rust Creek Falls, all the brides flocked to the old train depot to get Viv to create their perfect wedding.

Unfortunately, both the rustic train depot and Viv's primary local wedding venue—the brick freight house nearby—needed new roofs. All new. They couldn't just slap a fresh layer of shingles on. Both buildings required tear-outs and rebuilds. Plus, there were structural issues that would have to be addressed. Viv had collected bids. She knew what the work would cost.

It was a lot.

And the wedding planners had already stretched every penny to the limit.

Gently, Sarah laid it out. "I'm sorry. I've been over and over the numbers you gave me. The money just isn't there. You need a loan or an investor."

"A loan against what?" Viv was shaking her head. "The buildings and the land belong to Cole's family." Her husband, Cole Dalton, was a local rancher. Cole and his large extended family owned a lot of the land in the Rust Creek Falls Valley. "I can't take a loan against my in-laws' property. We're doing great, but, Sarah, you already know it's all on a shoestring—and frankly, I struck out on my own so that I could do this *my* way." Viv's big green eyes shone with sheer determination. "An investor is going to want a say in how we run things."

"Not necessarily. Some investors just want a percentage of—"

The little bell over the front door cut Sarah off midsentence.

"Good morning, ladies," boomed a deep male voice. The imposing figure in the open doorway swept off his black Stetson to reveal a thick head of silver hair. "Maximilian Crawford, at your service." The man plunked his big hat to his heart. Tall and powerfully built, with a handsome, lived-in face and a neatly trimmed goatee and mustache, the guy almost didn't seem real. He reminded Sarah of a character from one of those old-time TV Westerns. "I'm looking for Vivienne Dalton, the wedding planner," he announced.

"I'm Viv." Viv started to step out from behind the worktable.

But Maximilian was faster. In five giant strides, he was at her side. He took Viv's hand and kissed it. "Such a pleasure to meet you. I've heard great things." He turned to Caroline, kissed her hand and then took Sarah's and brushed his mustache across the back of it, too.

Viv, who'd looked slightly stunned when the older man bowed over her hand, recovered quickly and made introductions. "Maximilian, this is Caroline, my partner, and Sarah Turner, with Falls Mountain Accounting."

"So happy to meet you, all three of you—and please

call me Max. My sons and I have bought the Ambling A Ranch east of here. We're newly arrived from the Dallas area, but we have Crawford relatives here in Rust Creek Falls. We're putting down roots in your fine community."

"Welcome to town, Max." Viv cut to the point. "How can we help you?"

"I have an important job that needs doing. And, Vivienne, I know you are the one to tackle it."

"Well, if it's a wedding you're after, you've come to the right place. I take it you're the groom?"

Max threw back his silver head and let out a booming laugh. "Sorry, Viv. Not me. I've had enough of wedded bliss to last me three lifetimes. But my boys are another story. I've got six, each one better lookin' than the one before. Goodhearted, my boys, if a bit skittish on the subject of love and marriage. As we speak, all six are single." He shook a finger. "You ask me, that goes against the laws of God and man. It's about time my boys settled down."

Caroline wore a puzzled frown. "So, then, what you're saying is that all six of your sons are engaged?"

Max let out a low, rueful chuckle. "No, pretty lady. What I'm saying is that my boys need brides. And, Viv, that's where you come in. I want you and the lovely Caroline here to find each of my boys the perfect woman to marry—for a price, of course. A very nice price."

A silence followed. A long one. Sarah, who'd moved back from the worktable to let the wedding planners do their stuff, couldn't help wondering if maybe Max Crawford was a few bucking broncs short of a rodeo.

And judging by their carefully neutral expressions, Viv and Caroline also had their doubts.

However, the train depot roofs weren't going to replace themselves. Viv needed a large infusion of cash, stat. And if Max *was* for real, cash was exactly what he offered—too bad he was ordering up services Caroline and Viv didn't provide.

"But, Max," Viv said patiently, "we *plan* weddings. We aren't matchmakers."

"And why not? Matchmaking is an honest, time-honored practice. A lucrative one, too—at least it will be for you, with me as your client."

Viv slowly shook her head. "I'm so sorry. But we just don't—"

"A million," Max cut in, bringing a trio of stunned gasps from Viv, Caroline and Sarah, too. Max nodded at Viv. "You heard me right. A million dollars. You find my boys wives and the money is yours."

"Max." Viv let out a weak laugh. "That's just crazy."

"That's where you're wrong. I've made my fortune thinking outside the box. And that makes me living, breathing proof that anything can be achieved if you're willing to make your own rules."

Sarah took another step back from the worktable. She couldn't have disagreed more. Rules mattered. And as much as she would like for Max to be the solution to Viv's money troubles, fast-talking men were dangerous. Sarah had learned that sad lesson the hard way.

Viv wasn't going for it, either. "Are you asking us to set up six arranged marriages? No. Definitely not. Caroline and I could never do that."

"Arranged?" Max huffed out a breath. "No way.

My boys would never go for that. They'll choose their own brides. All I'm asking is that you find the perfect woman for each of them."

"Right," Viv scoffed. "Easy peasy."

"Love isn't something you can force." Caroline added her quiet voice to Viv's mocking one. "It really does have to develop naturally and—"

"Caroline, darlin'." Max patted her shoulder. "I couldn't agree with you more. We're on the same page. You won't be *arranging* anything. You won't need to. I've heard all about Rust Creek Falls. Love is everywhere you turn around here and the percentage of pretty women is satisfyingly high. You set my boys up and they are bound to fall."

Sarah took another step back. How could they believe a word the guy said? He talked too fast and he'd openly admitted that he made his own rules.

As if he'd sensed her retreat, the big man shifted his glance to Sarah. "So how 'bout you, darlin'?"

Sarah straightened her shoulders and hitched up her chin. "What about me?"

"Are you looking for the right guy to marry?"

She was looking for anything but. "Excuse me? You want to marry me off to one of your sons?"

"Sweet, sweet Sarah, just say yes." Max actually winked at her. "You won't regret it."

"Sorry, but I'm not on the, um, market."

"Got a sweetheart already, then?"

"No. I'm simply not interested."

Max heaved a big sigh. "That's a crying shame, and I mean that sincerely. You're a beautiful woman with a sharp brain, I can tell. You'd be just perfect for—"

"Dad. What are you up to now?" At the sound of another commanding male voice, Sarah whirled toward the open door.

"Patience, Logan," Max replied. "Just give your old man a few minutes more."

"They plan weddings here, Dad. You don't have a fiancée, so you don't need a wedding. Xander and I are getting tired of waiting in the truck."

Sarah tried not to stare. But really, who could blame her? The cowboy in the doorway was hot—tall and lean, with thick brown hair and a mouth that would have just about any girl thinking of long, scorching kisses.

At the moment, though, that gorgeous mouth was scowling at Max. "What's going on here?"

As he spoke, another fine-looking cowboy entered behind him. The second guy said, "Whatever you think you're pulling, Dad—don't."

Max only laughed. "Come on over here, boys. Let me introduce you to Viv, Caroline and Sarah." His big white teeth gleamed as his smile stretched wide again. "What did I tell you, ladies? Meet my oldest son, Logan, and third-born, Xander."

The first cowboy, Logan, flicked a glance in Sarah's direction—and froze. Now he was staring right at her. "Hello, Sarah," he said low. Intimately. As though they were the only two people in the room.

And then he was on the move again, coming straight for her. He stopped a foot away, right up in her space. The breath fled her lungs. The guy was even hotter up close. It should be illegal to have eyes so blue.

With a little shiver of unwelcome delight, she took

his offered hand. His big, warm fingers engulfed hers. More shivers skittered up her arm.

Absurd. Sarah Turner had no time for the shivers. Not anymore. No way was she letting a pair of bedroom eyes lead her astray again.

But Logan wasn't making it easy for her. He stared at her like she was the most beautiful creature he'd ever seen.

Why? She so didn't get it. She was not at her best and hadn't been for way too long now. A year and a half ago, she'd been hot…ish.

Now, though? She wore her hair in a ponytail to keep it out of the way and didn't bother with makeup beyond a swipe of mascara and maybe some lip gloss. On a good day, she made it all the way to dinnertime without getting spit-up on her shirt.

Max just kept talking. "Boys, Viv and Caroline here not only plan weddings, they also serve as the Rust Creek Falls dating service." Such a liar, that Max. He wouldn't know the truth if it bit him on the butt. "And Sarah is not only gorgeous—she's got a mind for figures, works as an accountant right in town. Falls Mountain Accounting, I believe. Have I got that right, Sarah?"

Logan still held her hand. She really ought to pull away. But she didn't. "I'm a CPA, yes," she said as she continued to stare into Logan's blue eyes.

"I think I need an accountant," said the killer-handsome cowboy in that deep, smooth voice of his, never once letting go of her gaze—or her hand. "And a dating service works for me. Sign me up. I'll take you, Sarah. To dinner. Tonight."

"Uh, yeah. Right." She laughed, playing it off, as her traitorous heart flipped cartwheels inside her chest.

Ridiculous. Impossible. She had no time for dates. If she had any extra time, she would spend it sleeping. And never again would she believe the lies of a handsome, smooth-talking man.

Max was still talking. "Sarah, Logan here is a self-made man. He grew up on our ranch in Texas, but he couldn't wait to get out on his own. Earned his fortune in Seattle, in real estate."

Logan chuckled. "Shut up, Dad."

Max didn't miss a beat. "Son, why don't you and Sarah go on into town? Take her to the donut shop. You can firm up your dinner plans over bear claws and coffee."

Sarah opened her mouth to give both father and son a firm no when a baby's cry from the back room did it for her.

"Huh?" Max blinked in surprise. "That sounds like a—"

"Excuse me." Sarah pulled her hand free of Logan's warm grip and managed a breezy smile. "My little girl wants her mother." Turning neatly on her heel, she headed for the back room.

Was she disappointed that a certain dreamboat of a man was bound to lose interest fast when faced with a crying baby?

A little, maybe. But not *that* disappointed.

Really, it was for the best.

Logan Crawford watched Sarah's bouncing ponytail as she trotted away from him. What was it about her?

Those big golden-brown eyes, all that shining bronze hair? That smile she had that was shy and devilish simultaneously? Damned if that smile didn't dare him to kiss her.

He would take that dare at the first opportunity.

Was she married?

He hadn't seen a ring—and yeah, the baby kind of gave him pause.

But not that much of a pause. He could work around the baby. As long as she was single, well, why shouldn't the two of them have a little fun? Nothing lasted forever and he liked it that way.

It was chemistry, pure and simple. Sexual attraction. And damn, it felt good.

His dad was still talking to the other two women, while Xander just stood there looking midway between vaguely intrigued and slightly annoyed by what they were saying.

Logan, on the other hand, felt downright invigorated. He hadn't felt like this in years. Maybe never. Lately, he'd been kind of off his game when it came to women. He just had no drive to hook up and hadn't been with anyone in months.

But everything had changed the minute he set eyes on Sarah.

Just let her be single. That was all he asked.

She emerged from the back room with a backpack-style diaper bag hanging off one shoulder, a giant leather tote dangling from one hand and a pouty-faced infant in a baby carrier on the other arm. "Sorry, everyone. We'll just be going."

Uh-uh. Not yet. In four strides, Logan reached her.

"Here. Let me help you." The baby stuck a fist in her mouth and stared up at him, wide-eyed.

"No, really." Sarah seemed flustered. Her cheeks had turned the sweetest shade of pink. "There's no need. I'm good."

He ignored her objections and eased the diaper bag off her shoulder. "What's her name?" He took hold of the tote. For a moment, she held on like she wouldn't let him take it.

But then she let go. "Sophia," she said. "Her name is Sophia."

"Pretty name. How old is she?" He wiggled his eyebrows at the baby, who had a pink cloth flower tied around her mostly bald head.

"Five months," said Sarah.

The baby took her slobbery hand out of her mouth long enough to announce, "Ah-da!" and stuck it right back in.

Behind him, his dad started flapping his jaws again, apologizing for trying to set them up. "I'm so sorry, Sarah. I didn't see a ring on your finger and I assumed—"

"You assumed right," Sarah responded coolly. "I'm not married."

Excellent. "But are you engaged?" Logan rattled off the pertinent questions. "Living with someone? Dating exclusively?"

"None of the above," she replied. "It's just me and Sophia." As if on cue, the little girl let out a goofy giggle around the fist in her mouth. Sarah added, delectably defiant, "Just us. And we like it that way."

So she's free. It was all Logan needed to know.

Unfortunately—and for no reason Logan could

understand—Max moved in next to him. "Son, Sarah has to go. Give her back her things."

Not happening. Not yet. "Give us a minute, would you, Dad?" He turned his back on his father and moved in closer to Sarah and little Sophia. That caused Sarah to retreat a step. Logan closed the distance. The process repeated—Sarah retreating, Logan eliminating the space she'd created—until they reached the door.

A glance over his shoulder revealed that Max had started talking to the wedding planners again. His dad and the blonde wedding planner shook hands. Logan made a mental note to find out what that was about as he turned his attention back to the irresistible brown-eyed girl.

She said, "I really do have to go."

Logan held on to her tote and diaper bag and started talking, pulling out all the stops, flirting shamelessly with both the woman and her baby. He made silly faces at Sophia as he coaxed information from Sarah, learning that she'd moved back to Rust Creek Falls a month before and had a cottage in town.

"Truly, Logan." Sarah's pretty white teeth nibbled nervously at her plump lower lip, driving him just a little bit crazy. He wanted to nibble on that lip himself. "I'm not interested in dating. I'm way too busy for anything like that."

He nodded. "I understand. Let me help you out to your car."

"No, that's not necessary."

"Yeah, it is. You've got too much to carry and I've got a couple of perfectly good free hands."

Her sweet mouth twisted with indecision—and then she gave up. "Well, um, okay. Thank you."

He walked her out to her white CR-V and waited while she strapped the baby's carrier in the back seat, handing her the giant bag and backpack when she was ready for them. She set them on the floor, shut the door and went around to the driver's door. Admiring the view, Logan followed after her.

"Well," she said with an overly bright smile as he held open the door for her. "Good luck, then—with the ranch and all."

"'Preciate that," he replied. She jumped in behind the wheel, her denim skirt riding up a little, giving him a perfect glimpse of one smooth, shapely thigh. "Drive safe," he said and shut the door.

She waved as she pulled out. He stood in the warm June sunlight, watching her drive away, thinking that he would be good for her, that she needed to get out and have some fun.

Sarah Turner deserved a little romance in her life and Logan Crawford was just the man to give her what she deserved.

Chapter Two

"Logan, it's a bad idea," his father said. "You need to forget about Sarah Turner."

It was past six that evening. Logan, his dad and Xander were out on the porch of the ranch house at the Ambling A enjoying a beer after spending a few hours plowing through the stacks of boxes that weren't going to unpack themselves. At some point, one of them needed to go inside and hustle up a meal. But for now, it was nice out and the beer was ice-cold and refreshing.

Logan stared off toward the snow-tipped mountains. The sky was cloudless, perfectly blue. "I like her, Dad. And it's not your call." He didn't point out that he was a grown-ass man and would do what he damn well wanted to do. Max ought to know that by now. "I'm curious, though. She's single, smart and pretty. She works for a living. She's got it all going on as far as I can see. What have you got against her?"

"Nothing," Max answered gruffly. "You're right. She seems like a fine person."

Xander rocked back in his chair and hoisted his boots up onto the porch rail. "So what's the problem then, Dad? I was standing right there when you struck that crazy deal with the wedding planners to find us all brides for a cool million bucks. To me, that means you want us all to get married. Whether that's ever gonna happen is another question entirely. But the way I see it, if Logan's found a girl already, you should count your blessings."

A million dollars to marry them off? Logan hadn't heard that part. Sometimes his dad came up with the wildest ideas. Logan had no plans to marry anybody. But that wasn't the point. He followed Xander's lead. "Yeah, Dad. You were eager enough to hook Sarah and me up until the baby started crying."

Max sipped his beer. "I do want you boys married. It's about damn time. But when kids are involved, well, things get too complicated." He pointed his longneck at Logan. "Take my word for it, son. You don't need that kind of trouble. Viv will find you someone perfect—someone sweet and pretty without a baby hanging off her hip."

"I'll say it again, Dad. *I* like Sarah and I'm going to move on that."

"I don't want you—"

"Stop. Listen. There is no problem here. You don't want me marrying Sarah Turner? Great. I'm not going to marry her—or anyone. The last thing I want right now is a wife, with or without a baby in the bargain, so you can save that million bucks. When my time comes to tie the knot—if it ever does—I'll find my own bride. I don't need anyone setting me up."

Xander recrossed his boots on the railing. "That's too bad. Because Dad's got that wedding planner setting us *all* up."

Logan leveled a warning look on his dad. "Are you listening? Because you ought to know your own sons better than that. I think I can speak for all six of us when I say that we're not letting anyone choose brides for us—not you, Dad, and not those two wedding planners back at the train depot."

"Nobody's choosing for you," Max insisted. "Viv and Caroline are just going to be introducing you to some lovely young single ladies. You should thank me for making it so easy for you to develop social connections in our new hometown."

Xander grunted. "Social connections? You're kind of scaring me now, Dad."

"I just don't get it," Logan said to Max. "For years, you've been going on about how marriage is a trap—and now suddenly you're shelling out a million bucks to make sure we've each got a wife?"

"Yeah." Xander scowled. "Seriously, Dad. You need to cut that crap out."

"Don't get on me, boys." Max assumed a wounded expression, but he didn't say he would give up his matchmaking scheme.

Not that Logan really expected him to. Unfortunately, once Maximilian Crawford got an idea in his head, telling him to cut it out wouldn't stop him.

They would have to warn their brothers that Max had brokered a marriage deal for all of them and they shouldn't be surprised to find a lot of "lovely single ladies" popping up every time they turned around.

Just then, a quad cab rolled into the yard. A tall, solidly built cowboy got out.

Max stood from his chair. "Nate Crawford. Thanks for coming."

The guy did have that Crawford look about him—strong and square-jawed. He joined them on the porch. Max offered him a beer. They made small talk for a few minutes.

Nate, Logan learned, was a mover and shaker in Rust Creek Falls. He owned controlling interest in the upscale hotel just south of town called Maverick Manor. Logan thought Nate seemed a little reserved. He couldn't tell for sure whether that was because Nate was just one of those self-contained types—or because Max's reputation had preceded him.

Logan loved his dad, but Max was no white knight. The man was a world-class manipulator and more than a bit of a scamp. Yeah, he'd made himself a fortune over the years—but there was no doubt he'd done more than one shady deal.

Yet people were drawn to him. Take Logan and his brothers. They were always complaining about Max's crazy schemes. Yet somehow Max had convinced each one of them to make this move to Montana.

For Logan, it was partly a matter of timing. He'd been between projects in Seattle and ready for a change. When Max had offered a stake in a Montana cattle ranch, Logan had packed his bags and headed for Big Sky Country.

If nothing else, he'd thought it would be good for him to get some time with his brothers. And yeah, he couldn't help wondering what wild scheme his dad might be cooking up now.

Never in a thousand years would Logan have guessed that Max had decided to marry them all off.

Max clapped Nate on the shoulder. "I really do appreciate your dropping by. Wanted to touch base, you know? Family does matter, after all. And now that me and the boys are settling in the area, we'd like to get to know you and everyone else in the family here."

"How about this?" Nate offered. "Saturday night. Dinner at Maverick Manor. The Rust Creek Falls Crawfords will all be there."

"That'll work," said Max. "My other four boys will be up from Texas with the breeding stock by then. Expect all seven of us."

"Looking forward to it." Nate raised his beer and Max tapped it with his.

The next morning at nine sharp, Logan paid a visit to Falls Mountain Accounting.

The door was unlocked, so he walked right in.

Inside, he found a deserted waiting room presided over by an empty front desk with a plaque on it that read, Florence Turner, Office Manager. The door with Sarah's name on it was wide open. No sign of his favorite accountant, though.

The door next to Sarah's was shut. The nameplate on that one read Mack Turner, Accountant. Something was going on inside that office. Faintly, Logan heard muffled moans and sighs.

A woman's voice cried softly, "Oh, yes. Yes, my darling. Yes, my love. Yes, yes, yes!"

Logan debated whether to turn and run—or stick around just to see who emerged from behind that door.

Wait a minute. What if it was Sarah carrying on in there?

It had damn well better not be.

He dropped into one of the waiting room chairs—and then couldn't sit still. Rising again, he tossed his hat on the chair and paced the room.

What was this he was feeling—like his skin was too tight and he wanted to punch someone?

Jealousy?

Not happening. Logan Crawford had never been the jealous type.

He was…curious, that's all, he reassured himself as he marched back to his chair, scooped up his hat and sat down again.

The sounds from behind the shut door reached a muted crescendo and finally stopped.

A few minutes later, a flushed, dewy-eyed older woman who looked quite a bit like Sarah emerged from Mack Turner's office. Her brown hair needed combing and her silky shirt was half-untucked.

"Oh!" Her blush deepened as she spotted Logan. "I, um…" She tugged in her shirt and patted at her hair. "I'm so sorry. Just, um, going over the calendar for the day. I'm Florence Turner."

Hiding his grin, he rose again. She marched straight for him, arm outstretched.

"Logan Crawford," he said as they shook.

"Please just call me Flo. I manage the office. We're a family business, just my husband, our daughter, Sarah, and me." Flo put extra heavy emphasis on the word *husband*. Apparently, she wanted to make it perfectly clear that whatever he'd heard going on behind Mack Turner's door was sanctioned by marriage. "Are you here to see Mack?"

"I'm waiting for Sarah."

"Oh! Did you have an appointment?"

"Not exactly." He tried a rueful smile.

"Well, I apologize for the mix-up, but Sarah has meetings with clients—all day, I think she said."

"Really? That's inconvenient." He patted his pockets. "I seem to have lost my phone." He'd left it in the truck, but Flo didn't need to know that.

"Oh, I'm so sorry," Sarah's mom said.

"Unfortunately, that means now I don't have Sarah's cell number..." Okay, yeah. He'd never had a cell number for her. But it was only a *little* lie.

And it worked like a charm. Flo whipped out Sarah's business card. It had her office, home and cell numbers on it.

"You're a lifesaver. Thank you."

"Any time, Logan—and you're more than welcome to use the phone on my desk."

"Uh, no. I need a coffee. I'll use the pay phone at the donut shop up the street."

That was another lie. He called her from his truck as soon as he was out of sight of Falls Mountain Accounting.

* * *

Sarah was with a client when the call came in from an unknown number. She let it go straight to voice mail. The day was a busy one, appointments stacked up one after the other.

When she finally checked messages in the late afternoon, she found one from Logan.

"Hello, Sarah. It's Logan Crawford. Call me back when you get a minute."

She played it through twice, sitting in her white CR-V with Sophia snoozing in the back seat. His voice, so calm and commanding, made her feel strangely breathless.

The truth was, she hadn't been able to stop thinking of him, of the way he'd looked at her, like she was the only person in the room, of the way he'd kept hold of her hand when there was no excuse for him to be holding it beyond the fact that he wanted to. She'd loved how he'd been so sweet to Sophia and that he'd insisted on carrying her diaper bag and tote out to the car.

Plus, well, he was way too good-looking and she hadn't been with a man in over a year.

The plan was to give up men, after all. At least for a decade or so—maybe longer.

And really, hadn't she made her unavailability perfectly clear to him?

Annoyed and flustered and oddly gleeful all at the same time, she called him back.

"Hello, Sarah."

"Hi, Logan. How did you get my number?"

"I stopped by your office. Your mom gave me your

card." Dear Lord in heaven, his voice. It was so smooth, like raw honey. She pictured it pouring from a mason jar, all sweet and thick and slow. And then he added, "Your mom and dad are obviously very happy together."

Sarah felt her face go hot. Stifling an embarrassed groan, she answered drily, "Yeah. I try to be out of the office as much as possible." Then she changed the subject. "Logan, I'm flattered you went to all that trouble just to get my number, but really, I meant what I said. I hardly have time to wash my hair lately. I'm not dating anyone, not even you."

"I get it. I called on business."

"Oh." Did she sound disappointed? Well, she wasn't. Not at all.

He said, "We're just getting moved in at the Ambling A and frankly, the accounts are a mess. We need a professional to get the books on track. We want to hire local. And that means Falls Mountain Accounting."

Her heart rate had accelerated at just the idea of being near him as she gathered the information to whip those books of his into order—but no. She needed to keep her distance from him, which meant he would have to work with her dad. "Did you meet with my dad yet? He's the best. I know you'll be happy you hired him."

"Sarah." He made her name into a gentle reproach. "Your dad seems to have his hands full—with your mom."

She did groan then. "I do not believe you said that." He didn't immediately respond and she suddenly had a burning need to speak, fill the silence between them. Bad idea. But she did it anyway. "They never used to be like that, I swear. I don't know what happened. I haven't asked. I doubt I ever will."

"I understand."

"Yeah," she grumbled. "Sure, you do." He made a soft, amused sort of sound. "Did you just chuckle, Logan? I swear to God I heard you chuckle."

His answer was actually more of a demand. "*You*, Sarah. I intend to hire *you*." He was just so...commanding. She'd never liked bossy men, but she found herself longing to make an exception in his case. In a strictly professional sense, of course.

And she might as well be honest—at least with herself. It was a definite ego boost to have this hot rancher so interested in her, even if she would never let it go anywhere.

Plus, well, he'd insisted he wanted to work with her. If she said no, he would go elsewhere. It wasn't good for business to turn away work.

"All right, Logan. Have it your way."

"I love it when you say yes. How about I meet you at your office?"

Her office, where there was no telling what her parents might be up to? "Er, no. I'll come out to the Ambling A."

"That's even better. I feel I should warn you, though, it's kind of a mess, old records all over the place. Some are on floppy disks, believe it or not. There are even some dusty, leather-bound ledgers that go back to the fifties."

"It will be fine, don't worry. Mostly, I need the current stuff."

"Well, I've got that, too."

She quoted her hourly rate.

"That works. Today?"

"Logan, it's almost five. I need to go home, feed my baby, maybe even stretch out on the sofa and veg out to the new season of *GLOW*."

"You're tired." He actually sounded as though he cared. "Tomorrow, then."

"All right. I have a nine o'clock that should go for an hour, two tops. After that, I'm flexible. Is it all right if I call you when I'm ready to head over to the Ambling A?"

"Works for me. Call me on this number."

She said goodbye and then sat behind the wheel for a moment, thinking how she would have to watch herself tomorrow, make sure she kept things strictly business. In the back seat, Sophia made a soft, happy sound in her sleep, and that had Sarah thinking how good Logan was with the baby.

Too good, really. The last thing she needed was him being charming and wonderful with Sophia. That could weaken her already shaky defenses.

Sarah bent her head over her phone again and texted her dearest friend since childhood, Lily Hunt.

Hey. You on the job at the Manor tomorrow?

Lily was an amazing cook and worked at Maverick Manor as a part-time chef.

Not tomorrow. Why?

Now, that was a long story. One she didn't really want to get into via text—or in a phone call *or* face-to-face. Because what was there to say, really? Nothing had happened between her and Logan and nothing was *going* to happen.

I have to go visit a new client, Logan Crawford. He and his dad and five brothers have bought the Ambling A. I think things will go more smoothly if I'm not trying to take care of Sophia while I'm setting up their accounts. So how 'bout a cushy babysitting gig at my house?

There. That sounded simple and reasonable without giving away too much. She hit Send.

And Lily took it at face value: You're on. Tell Sophia that Aunt Lily can't wait. When to when?

Be at my place at 8:30. I should be back by two or three.

I'll be there. But I want something from you in return.

What? You think I won't pay you?

Sarah, I know you'll pay me. You always do. If I didn't take the money, you would chase me up Pine Street waving a handful of bills.

Very funny.

These are my terms. Saturday at 6. Dinner at the Manor. You and me, my treat. A girls' night out. We deserve it. Get your mom to take Sophia. That's what grandmas do. Come on, it will be fun.

It did sound kind of fun. Sarah hadn't been out to dinner in so long, she couldn't remember the last time. And Lily didn't get out enough either, really.

Sarah, I meant it. Ask your mom.

Grinning, Sarah replied, Okay. I'll ask her.

Yes! See you tomorrow morning, 8:30 sharp. And don't put it off, call your mom now.

Sarah did call her mom. Flo answered on the first ring. "Honey, I'm so glad you called. Here you are back in town and we're all working together—and yet, somehow, we hardly see you. How's my sweet grandbaby?"

"Asleep at the moment."

"She is an angel—oh, and by the way," her mom began much too coyly, "a handsome cowboy showed up at the office this morning looking for you."

Who are you and what have you done with my real mother? Sarah thought but didn't ask. Florence Turner used to be quiet and unassuming. A nice person, but a grim one. Not anymore. When she wasn't disappearing into her husband's office for a quickie, Flo bounced around Falls Mountain Accounting full of energy and big smiles. It had been that way since Sarah moved home from Chicago a month ago. Who knew when it had started?

Sarah was afraid to ask.

Her mom prompted, "Did he call you?"

"Logan Crawford, you mean?"

"That's him."

"Yes, he called me."

"Honey, that is one fine-looking hunk of a man, a complete hottie, I don't mind telling you."

"Yeah, I've seen him. Thanks, Mom."

"You should snap that one up."

"Mom. He wants me to straighten out his accounts, that's all."

"Oh, I think he's hoping to have you *straighten out* a lot more than his accounts."

"Mom!"

"Sweetheart, don't be a prude. Life is beautiful and so are you. You deserve the best of everything—including a tall, hot cowboy with gorgeous blue eyes."

"Yes, well. I didn't call to talk about Logan. I was wondering if you would watch Sophia Saturday night. Lily and I want to get together for dinner."

"Honey, at last!"

"What do you mean by that?"

"You've been home for weeks and this is the first time you've asked me to take Sophia for you."

"Oh, well, I…" Sarah didn't know what to say. Her mom had offered, but it had never really been necessary.

"It's all right," Flo reassured her. "I'm just glad you've finally asked me—and yes, I would love to."

"Perfect." Sarah thanked her and ended the call before her mother could say another word about Logan Crawford and his hotness.

Armed with her laptop, her business tote and the steely determination not to be seduced by a sweet-talking cowboy, Sarah arrived at the Ambling A at eleven the next morning.

Logan was waiting for her on the long front porch

of the giant log-style house. He wore faded jeans that fit his strong legs much too perfectly and a dark blue shirt that clung to his lean chest and arms and brought out the color of his eyes. He dropped his hat on one of the porch chairs and came down the steps to open her car door for her.

"Where's Sophia?" he asked. She'd just picked up her laptop from the passenger seat. He reached in and took it from her, tucking it under his arm as he offered his hand to help her from her car.

She hardly required assistance to get out from behind the wheel and she really was trying not to let him get too close. But to refuse him just seemed rude.

"The baby?" he asked again as his warm, slightly rough fingers closed around hers. His touch felt way too good. She grabbed her giant leather tote with her free hand and hooked it over her shoulder.

"Sophia's at home today." She emerged from the car into the late-morning sunlight. "My friend Lily was free and agreed to babysit." They stared at each other.

His fine mouth twitched at one corner as he quelled a smile. "I'm disappointed. I was looking forward to another lively game of peekaboo."

Just like the other day at the train depot, she had to remind herself to ease her hand from his.

He led her inside, where there were moving boxes stacked in the front hall.

"It's a great house," she said, staring at the wide, rustic staircase that led up to a gallery-style landing on the second floor. "I vaguely remember the Abernathy family. They owned the place first and built the house, but they left a long time ago."

"We got a hell of a deal on the place from the last owners, I'll say that much." He put his hand on the fat newel post. "The house needs work, but we'll get around to that eventually. Right now, we're just trying to get everything unpacked—my dad and Xander and me. My other brothers will be showing up in the next couple of days. Then we'll be focused on buying more stock. The barn and stables need repair. Lot of ditches to burn and fences to mend. Fixing up the house is low on the list of priorities."

She should move things along, tell him she needed to get going on the work he had for her. But she was curious about him. "So, you're from Texas, I think your dad said?"

He nodded. "We had a ranch near Dallas. Me and my brothers grew up there."

"You *had* a ranch?"

"We put it on the market when we decided on the move here."

"So, you've always been a rancher, huh?"

He shook his head. "I went to college for a business degree and then moved to Seattle. Been there ever since."

"Seattle." She remembered then. "That's right. Your dad said you were in real estate."

"Property development, to be specific. I got there just in time for the boom years, and I did well. But then my dad got this wild hair to move to Montana, get us all together working a new spread. The timing was right for me. I'd been thinking that I was ready to try something different." He was looking at her so steadily. She liked having his gaze focused on her. She liked it way too much.

Then he asked, "How 'bout you? Where did you go to college? Have you always lived in Rust Creek Falls?"

His questions were perfectly reasonable.

Her response took her completely by surprise.

All of a sudden, her throat was too tight and there was pressure behind her eyes.

Really, what was the matter with her? Out of nowhere, she hovered on the verge of bursting into tears, right here in the front hall of the Ambling A ranch house with this too-handsome, charming man looking on.

Crying? Seriously? She wasn't a cryer. Crying was pointless and completely uncalled-for in this situation.

And yet still, she wanted to put her head in her hands and bawl like a baby over all the ways her life hadn't turned out as she'd planned, just stand here sobbing right in front of this superhot guy. A guy who seemed hell-bent on seducing an overworked, constantly exhausted single mom who wanted nothing more to do with the male of the species, thank you very much.

She gulped the ludicrous tears down and managed an answer. "I went to Northwestern and then I worked in Chicago for a while."

Now he was frowning at her, a worried sort of frown. Those eyes of his seemed to see way too much. "Sarah, are you okay?"

"I'm fine." She pasted on a wobbly smile. "Really. And don't you have a mountain of records and receipts to show me?"

He gave her a long look, a look both considering and concerned, as though he was trying to decide whether to push her to confess what was bothering her or back off. She breathed a sigh of relief when he said, "Right this way."

They went down a central hallway, past a big living room and a kitchen that could use a redo to an office at the back of the house.

By then, she'd pulled herself together. "You weren't kidding." She gave a low laugh as she approached the big mahogany desk that dominated the room, its surface piled with old ledgers, dusty CDs and floppies.

"Most of this is probably meaningless to us, I realize," he said, setting her laptop on a side chair.

She put her tote down beside it. "Yeah, it's doubtful I'll need any of the records generated by the former owners."

"If you don't need them, we can just toss them out."

"I *might* need them. I can't say until I look through all the current records. And *you* might want to look through it all later. You might find out you own something you didn't even know you bought."

"Even the floppies? They would need converting just to read them, wouldn't they?"

She shrugged. "Doesn't hurt to keep them for a while. If you decide at some point you want to go through them, we have a guy in Kalispell who will convert them for you."

"That sounds really exciting." He put on a dazed expression, even crossing his eyes. His playfulness made her grin and caused a flare of warmth in her belly. The man was way too appealing. But at least she was no longer about to cry and he'd stopped looking worried that she might have a meltdown right in front of him.

She said, "What I'll need to set you up are your current records, including whatever you've got up till now of the Ambling A's inventory, income and expenses."

"Income?" He chuckled. "Not hardly. Not yet."

"Well, okay then. Just your expenses and whatever inventory you have of machinery, equipment and livestock—including your best judgment of their value. I'll need the documents you received from the title company when you closed the sale. I'll put it all together using a basic accounting program that should be easy to keep current. That will be a few days to a week of work for me here at the ranch, if that's all right?"

"Sounds good to me." He had that look, like he was talking about a lot more than bookkeeping.

She pretended not to notice what a shameless flirt he was. "I'll be in and out because I need to keep up with my other clients, too. But if I do the work here, I can come right to you with any questions I have about the records you've given me. We can clear up any issues on the spot."

"Works for me." He said it in a low rumble that stirred a bunch of butterflies to life in her belly.

She tried valiantly to keep a professional tone as she rattled off more suggestions. "After you're all set up, you'll need someone to post transactions regularly. I have a couple of local people who can do that. Or you can just put in the time every week or so and do it yourself. I suggest you reconcile the bank balance and the general ledger at least once a month."

"Sure. And I'll hire whoever you suggest. What about tax time?" he asked.

"I'll be happy to do your taxes."

"Good." He arched an eyebrow and teased, "How 'bout an audit?"

She laughed. "Very funny. You know I can't audit my own work."

"Damn. Busted." He tipped his head to the side, his gaze lazy and warm. It felt so good just to have him looking at her, to be staring right back at him, thinking all kinds of naughty thoughts as she went through her stock suggestions for keeping accounts in order.

Really, this was getting out of control. They were more or less having sex with their eyes. If she didn't watch out, she would do something crazy, like throw herself into his arms and beg him to kiss her.

Uh-uh. It needed to stop.

"I should get to work," she said.

"Right." He pointed at the piled-high desk. "I think everything you need is there, including that big manila folder jammed with receipts, the inventory lists and the packet from the title company. You can tell the current stuff by the lack of dust."

"Okay, then." She moved behind the desk and pushed the records she would be using to one side. That left the piles of ledgers and old disks.

He got the message. "You need space to work."

"Do you have another desk you want me to use? A table works fine, too."

"The desk is yours for as long as you need it. I'll box up the old records, get them out of your way."

There were empty boxes waiting against one wall. Together, they started putting the ledgers in one box and piling the old disks in another.

She'd straightened from the boxes and was turning

to the desk to grab another handful of disks when she spotted Max leaning in the open doorway to the back hall. He looked like some old-time gunslinger in black jeans, black boots, a white shirt and a black Western-cut jacket.

"The lovely Sarah," the older man said. "What a surprise." Something in his tone made her uneasy, some faint edge of…what? Mistrust? Disapproval?

But why?

"Hi, Max." She gave him a big smile.

He didn't smile back or even give her a nod, but turned to Logan as though she wasn't even there. "Give me a few minutes?"

"Can't it wait? Sarah and I were just—"

"Go." Sarah faked an offhand tone. She felt completely dismissed by Max and that had her emotions seesawing again the way they had in the front all. There was absolutely no reason she should care if Logan's dad didn't like her. But she did care. There was a clutch in her throat and a burning behind her eyes as her totally inappropriate tears threatened to rise again. She waved Logan off. "Talk to your dad. I'll finish clearing the desk and get to work."

Impatient to return to his favorite accountant, Logan reluctantly followed Max out to the back porch.

The old man leaned on one of the posts that framed the steps down to the yard. He stared out at the ragged clumps of wild bunchgrass that extended to the back fence. Like too many fences on the property, it needed repair.

Logan braced a shoulder against the other post.

"Okay, Dad. What's so important we have to deal with it right this second?"

Max's gaze remained on the backyard. He took a long count of ten to answer. "I can see now why you suddenly decided we needed to get the books in order."

Why deny it? "You know I like Sarah. It shouldn't be a surprise—and we do need someone to set up a system to keep track of everything."

"You've got a fancy business degree. You can do all that yourself."

"Dad, I didn't come to Montana to take up bookkeeping. Sarah is equipped to do it fast and efficiently."

Max slanted him a narrow look. "Maybe you don't trust your old dad. You think you need a professional to tell you that everything's on the up-and-up."

Logan snorted out a dry laugh. "Oh, come on. I wouldn't have signed on for this if I thought you were up to something you shouldn't be. Still, it never hurts to have a professional putting a good system in place, keeping everyone honest."

"So you're telling me she's only here for her bookkeeping skills? You've got absolutely no interest in those big amber eyes and that pretty smile?"

This conversation was a complete waste of time— time he could be spending with the woman he couldn't stop thinking about. "I'm thirty-three years old," Logan said flatly, "long past the age I have to run my personal choices by you. I'll date who I want to date." *At least, I will if I can somehow convince Sarah to give me a shot.*

"A woman with a child, Logan. It's a bad idea. If it doesn't work out, the kids are always the ones who suffer."

Logan had had about enough. He straightened from

the porch post and turned to face his father directly. "What is it with you all of a sudden? Are you talking about Sheila?" Sheila was his mother. She'd left them when Logan was seven. It had taken him several years to accept that she was no mother to him in any way that mattered. Even saying her name made a bitter taste in his mouth. Max shot him a bleak glance, but then, without a word, he turned and stared off toward the fence again.

"You dragged me out here," Logan prodded. "Talk. I'm listening."

But Max only waved a dismissive hand and continued to stare at nothing. Fed up with him, Logan went back in the house.

When he entered the office, Sarah glanced up sharply from behind the desk. He didn't like the look on her face, a tense look, kind of teary-eyed, a look a lot like the one she'd had in the front hall earlier.

He pushed the door shut behind him. If Max had more to say, he could damn well knock. "What's wrong?"

She had her laptop open and the big packet of sale documents spread out in front of her. Shutting the laptop, she rose. "You know what? I should go." She swiftly lined up the stack of papers and closed the packet. "I know of a perfectly good bookkeeper in Kalispell. I'll text you his number."

"Sarah."

She didn't answer, just scooped up her laptop and took a step out from behind the desk. Logan stopped her by blocking her path, causing her to clutch the laptop to her chest and stare up at him defiantly. "Excuse me, please."

"Sarah."

She hitched up her pretty chin. "You are in my way."

"What's the matter?" It took everything he had not to touch her, not to grab her good and tight in his arms. "Talk to me."

Her soft lips trembled. "It's, um, quite obvious that your dad doesn't want me here."

"It's not about you, not really."

"Of course you would say that."

"Look. Sometimes I don't think *he* knows what he wants. He gets these wild ideas, that's all. You can't take him seriously. Bottom line, we need the accounts in order and that means we need *you*."

"But I just don't understand. It's like he thinks I'm after you or something, trying to trap you into—I don't know, putting a ring on my finger, I guess. And I'm not. I swear I'm not. I've got no interest in marriage. I don't want to trap anyone." She stared up at him through eyes swimming in barely held-back tears, so earnest, so very sincere. "Especially not, um, you."

He tried to tease her. "You know, if you keep talking that way, you're bound to hurt my feelings. I'm a very sensitive guy." And he did dare to touch her then. Clasping her shoulders, he held her gaze.

"I…oh, Logan." She looked absolutely miserable and he should probably just let her go. But he held on.

What *was* it that she did to him? He didn't get it. He felt like ten kinds of selfish jerk to be putting her through this. But still, he just stood there, hands holding her slim shoulders, keeping her in place.

Finally, she spoke again. "See, the thing is, it hasn't worked out for me, to get involved with a man. So I promised myself I wouldn't. Not for years. Maybe never.

And then you show up and, well, frankly, Logan, you really tempt me."

This was *bad* news? "Excellent."

"No. No, it's not. It's not excellent in the least. All it does is confuse me to feel this way about you. I don't need it, all this confusion. I'm already overworked and exhausted. The last thing I need is a sexy cowboy in the mix."

"Hold on," he said tenderly. "So then, what you're saying is you think I'm tempting and sexy?"

She huffed out a frustrated breath. "That is so not the point."

"Maybe not. But you can't blame me for being pleased to hear how you feel." He wanted to kiss her, just pull her close and put his mouth on hers. But he wasn't sure how she would react to that. She seemed really upset and he didn't want to make her any more so.

"It's all too much, don't you get it?" she cried. "I'm just plain on overload." And then, as if to illustrate her point, a single tear got away from her. It slipped over the dam of her lower eyelid and traced a gleaming trail down her cheek.

"Sarah. Damn it." He let her go, but only so he could get his hands on the laptop she clutched so tightly. When he tried to take it, she resisted. "It's okay," he coaxed. "Come on, now. Let go." And she did. When she gave in and released it, he plunked it down on the desk and took her shoulders again. "Sarah, don't cry."

Another tear escaped. And another after that. "Too late," she said in a tiny voice.

"Aw, Sarah…" He pulled her close and she let him,

collapsing against him, her soft arms sliding around his waist.

For a too-short span of perfect seconds, she clung to him. He breathed in the clean scent of her silky hair, wondered what she'd done to him, hoped that whatever it was, she would never stop.

But then she looked up again, her eyes wet and so sad, a tear dripping off the end of her pretty nose.

"Here," he said. "Sit down." He pushed her gently back into the old leather desk chair and looked around for a tissue. There weren't any.

She sniffled. "Give me my tote, please." He went around the desk to grab it from the chair where she'd left it and handed it to her. She pulled out a travel pack of tissues, took one and wiped the tears from her cheeks. "I'm a mess," she said.

"No." A hank of her hair had escaped from her ponytail. Gently, he guided it back behind the shell of her ear. Retreating, but only a little, he hitched a leg up on the corner of the desk. "You're tired and overworked. And completely gorgeous."

She gave a little snort-sniffle at that. "Yeah, right."

He put up a hand, like a witness about to swear to tell the truth and nothing but the truth. "You're gorgeous," he said again. "And I mean that sincerely."

She started to smile, but couldn't quite manage it. Her shoulders slumped. "I'm just so tired, you know? Tired of working nonstop and trying to be a decent mom to Sophia and really not doing either all that well. I don't get it, I really don't. How did everything go so wrong?"

He leaned closer. "What went wrong? Sarah, come

on. Tell me. I need to know everything that's bothering you."

She scoffed. "Why?"

"So I can try to make it better." He actually meant that, he realized as he said it. He wanted to be with her—for as long as it lasted. And during that time, he wanted to be good for her. When they parted, he wanted her to remember him as a good guy who had treated her well.

She shook her head slowly. "If you keep pushing, I'm just going to go ahead and unload it all on you. My whole life story, all the ways I messed up. It will be a lot. It will be a really bad case of extreme oversharing and you will wish you'd never asked."

"No, I won't."

She scoffed. "Yes, you will. Believe me. Let's talk about something else."

"Uh-uh. For you to talk to me about what made you cry is exactly what I want." And he did want it. He really did. "Tell me. Tell me everything."

She stared at him, considering. "You're sure?"

"I am. Talk to me, please."

"Logan, I—"

He stopped her with a shake of his head. "Tell me."

For a long moment, she just stared at him. And then, at last, she let it all out.

Chapter Three

"My parents used to be so different," Sarah began.

Logan thought of Flo Turner the day before, coming out of her husband's office with her shirt untucked, her hair sticking out on one side and a smile of complete satisfaction on her flushed face. "How so?"

"When I was growing up, they were both so gloomy, always bleak and determined."

"You're not serious."

"As an IRS audit," she sneered. "They got married because they 'had to.'" She air-quoted that. "Because I was on the way. And they stayed married out of a sense of duty—they actually used to say that, how they stayed together because it was their duty. They were so noble. I couldn't wait to get out of that house, to live my own life, make things happen, get out in the big world and have everything. Success. True love. A great marriage.

Kids. And a whole lot of fun. But somehow, once I was on my own, there just wasn't enough time for fun, you know?"

"Why not?"

"I'm really not sure. I guess, because the way they raised me did rub off on me at least a little. I was driven, a straight-A student. I got a scholarship to Northwestern and my parents covered everything the scholarship didn't. I had a full ride and was driven to get through college fast and get on with my life." She'd studied like crazy, she said, and spent all her free time building her résumé.

To get a head start on her accounting career, she began interning in her sophomore year. She'd crammed six years of college and work experience into four and passed the CPA exam at the very young age of twenty-two. By then, she was already working at Chicago's top accounting firm.

And up until then, she'd never had a serious boyfriend.

"I met Tuck Evans not long after I got my CPA license. He was so charming. He also had a good job and claimed to be crazy for me. He was my first and only love—or so I thought." They'd moved in together.

But two years later, Tuck was perfectly happy with the status quo. "He said he saw no reason for us to get married. He said that we had it all without the ring. To teach him a lesson, I moved out and waited for him to come crawling back to me." She fell silent.

He prompted, "And?"

"Didn't happen. Finally, I called him. He was sweet and good-natured as ever, saying how right I was to end it. Really, he said, it wasn't working out and we both knew it." She glared up at Logan defiantly. "I was such an idiot."

"No, you weren't. Tuck wasn't good enough for you. He did you a favor."

Sarah glared harder. Logan could see her sharp brain working, trying to find something objectionable about what he'd just said. She wanted a fight.

He wasn't going to give her one. "Go on," he said gently.

She blew out a breath—and continued. "The day after I called Tuck and he said how glad he was that he and I were over, I headed off for a big conference in Denver. When a handsome bachelor came on to me at the conference, I decided a rebound fling was just what I needed."

"This handsome bachelor got a name?"

"Mercer Smalls. Does it matter?"

"No," he said honestly. "You're right. His name doesn't matter." Except that Mercer Smalls was a ridiculous name for a man. But whatever the guy's name had been, Logan would have disliked him on principle. Not that he was actually in any position to judge. He'd enjoyed more than one fling himself. Way more. And a lot of one-night hookups, too.

"I spent the three nights of the conference with Mercer," she said. "When we parted, he promised to call, but he didn't."

"Good riddance." Logan kept his tone mild, but he had to grit his teeth to do it.

Sarah sighed. "I was philosophical about it. Those three nights with Mercer helped me realize that flings just aren't for me. I knew I wouldn't be doing that again." She fell silent.

He realized that he was maybe a little like her first boyfriend, Tuck. And like the guy at the conference, too. Out for a good time, not looking for anything too serious. She was making it painfully clear that having a fling with a guy wasn't for her—that right now, she didn't want a guy at all.

He should back off, walk away.

But the thing was, she really got to him. And he *would* do right by her, damn it. She needed fun—all the fun she'd never had yet. She needed a man who knew how to treat a woman like a queen. It might not be forever, but when it ended, she would be glad for what they'd shared. He could make certain of that, at least.

And the silence between them had stretched out too long.

He guessed. "Mercer Smalls is Sophia's father?"

She nodded. "I couldn't believe it when I found out I was pregnant. It wasn't like we hadn't used protection. We had. But the stick turned blue anyway."

"Does Mercer know?"

"Of course. I knew the city he lived in and the name of his firm, so I reached out to him. I didn't imagine he would go down on one knee or even that he might be the guy for me, but a man has a right to know when he's going to be a father."

"He absolutely does," Logan agreed. A man deserved to know about his child, to be a part of his kid's life— even if the man was a player named Mercer Smalls who'd said he would call and never did.

"But as it turned out," she said, "Mercer wasn't a bachelor, after all. He was married with children and wanted nothing to do with me or the baby I was going to have. I couldn't believe it," she muttered, her eyes full of shadows, her gaze far away. "My rebound fling was a cheating husband who denied his unborn child outright. He just wanted to sign off all responsibility for the baby and be left alone."

He thought of Sophia, with her goofy little grin and her baby sounds that seemed like real words to him. Mercer Smalls was ten kinds of douchebucket. And a damn fool, to boot. "You gave him what he asked for?"

"You bet I did. His loss, the schmuck."

"I'm guessing this is the part where you swore off men forever?"

"How did you know?" She troweled on the irony. "I decided I would forget men and love and all that. I would be a successful single mom—and, Logan, I tried. I really did."

But fighting her way up the corporate ladder in the big city wasn't compatible with tackling motherhood solo on a tight budget. "The cost of day care for an infant was through the roof and I just couldn't keep up the pace at work."

In the end, she'd accepted the inevitable and moved home to Rust Creek Falls. "It's great, it really is—or it should be." She swiped another tear away. "I've got this cute, cozy cottage my parents own and a job in the family business. I can take Sophia with me to work whenever I need to. I mean, things could be so much worse. My baby is the light of my life and my parents are here to help and support me. Right?"

He nodded on cue and then prompted, "But?"

"Well, you've heard about Homer Gilmore, haven't

you?" At his puzzled frown, she grinned through her tears. "Nobody's told you about Homer?"

When he shook his head, she launched into this story about a local eccentric who made moonshine that had everyone doing crazy stuff. A few years ago, at a wedding on the Fourth of July, Homer had spiked the wedding punch. People had danced in fountains, gotten in a whole bunch of crazy fights—and had sex. A lot of sex. So much sex that nine months after that wedding, Rust Creek Falls had actually experienced a baby boom.

"My point being," she said, "that sometimes I wonder if my mom and dad have somehow drunk the Homer Gilmore moonshine. I mean, you've been to the office. You've witnessed firsthand how they are now. Their marriage of grim duty has turned into something completely different. My mother and father have fallen in love."

And if Flo and Mack weren't doing it in the office, she said, they were suddenly heading out the door, going who-knew-where together.

"Not to visit clients, that's for sure," she grumbled. "So yeah. I'm back in my old hometown, still trying to be a good mom while putting in killer hours doing my best to catch up with the workload my parents are currently too busy *schtupping* to shoulder."

He looked at her sideways. "Did you just say *schtupping*?"

"*I did. And* I have no idea where that came from. I've never used that word before in my life." Her sweet mouth was trembling—and not with tears this time. She laughed out loud, tipping back in the chair, the sound free and open and so good to hear.

He just wanted to hold her, though he doubted she'd allow it.

Still, he had to try. Rising, he offered his hand. She put hers in it. He pulled her up and into his arms, guiding her head to rest on his shoulder.

They laughed together, holding on to each other, until he tugged on the end of her ponytail.

She looked up at him. "What?"

"Is that it? Is that everything?"

"Pretty much, yeah. I'm working nonstop and still somehow barely keeping up. I adore my baby, but I hate being constantly frazzled and frumpy."

He put a finger to her lips. They were so soft, those lips. He ached to kiss them. "You're not frumpy. Not in the least. You're beautiful and you're doing a great job and it's all going to work out."

She actually smiled at him. "I shouldn't believe a word you say. But you know what? I kind of love it. Because all this flattery and praise, well, I can use a little flattery at this point. I really, really can."

"Sarah." He touched her silky cheek. And she didn't even try to stop him.

She didn't stop him when he traced the perfect shape of her ear, either. Or when he put his finger under her pretty chin and lifted it a fraction higher. She smelled so good, like flowers and baby lotion and something else, some delicate spice.

And then she whispered his name so softly and just a little bit hesitantly, lifting her chin even higher, offering up those plump, tempting lips to him.

He took what she offered. Carefully, at first, not wanting to push her, he brushed his mouth back and forth across hers until she opened to him, her lips parting on a soft, hungry cry.

It was all the invitation he needed.

He went for it, settling his mouth more firmly on hers, smiling a little when she made a sweet humming sound.

Her body was pliant in his arms. Every inch of her felt just right, giving and womanly, soft where he was hard. He could kiss her forever.

But too soon, with a tiny moan, she lowered her chin and broke the perfect kiss. Suddenly shy, she pressed her face into the crook of his shoulder.

He kissed her temple, her hair, even gave a quick nip to her earlobe. That brought a giggle. She lifted her gaze to him again. They regarded each other. Her eyes were almost pure gold right now.

"Let me take you out," he said. "Friday night. There's this great little Italian place in Kalispell I discovered a week or so ago when I got tired of eating Xander's cooking."

"Really, Logan. Didn't you hear a word I said?"

"I heard *every* word. Let me take you out."

"I just can't."

He touched her chin again, ran his thumb back and forth across those perfect, kissable lips of hers. "*Can't* has got nothing to do with it. You know you *can*. All you have to do is say yes."

"You are the sweetest man."

Sweet? Had any woman ever called him that? Doubtful. And he wasn't sure he liked it all that much. But he'd take it if it got him what he wanted. What they *both* wanted. Because she was drawn to him as much as he was to her. If he'd had any doubts on that score, the kiss they'd just shared had ended them. "So that's a yes, right?"

Her head went from side to side, that ponytail swaying slowly. "I've got no time for fancy restaurants."

"The restaurant I'm thinking of is a great place, but not that fancy, I promise you."

She sighed. "Logan, I shouldn't have kissed you and nothing is going to happen between us."

What was it about this woman? He'd never worked so hard to get a girl to say yes—and not even a yes to spending the night in his bed. Uh-uh. So far, he couldn't even convince her to let him buy her dinner.

He should give up.

But she had those golden eyes and she smelled so good and, well, something about her had him willing to do whatever he had to do just to get the raw beginnings of a chance with her. "How 'bout a quiet evening at your house, just you and me and little Sophia? I'll bring takeout."

"Really, I—"

"Yes." He said it firmly. "That's the word you're looking for. Three little letters. Just say it. Say it now."

"Oh, but I—"

"Yes. Come on, you can do it."

"Logan, you—"

"Yes."

"I—"

"Yes."

She bit her lower lip, adorably torn.

"Yes," he whispered yet again, holding her gaze nice and steady, keeping his tone gentle but firm.

And finally, she gave in and gave him what they both wanted. "Oh, all right. Friday night, takeout at my house. Yes."

The next day, Thursday, Logan's other four brothers arrived from Texas bringing a caravan of stock trailers full of horses and cattle. Sarah drove up not long after they all pulled in and Logan made the introductions.

Once she'd greeted them all, Sarah retreated to the office and got to work. That day and the next were busy ones at the ranch, what with getting the stock and the rest of the family settled in. Logan didn't have a lot of free time.

But for Sarah, he *made* time. He really liked the simple fact of her being there at the Ambling A, of knowing that he could see her whenever he had a spare minute or two. All he had to do was visit the office at the back of the house.

Both days, she brought Sophia with her. The baby slept in her carrier on the edge of the desk or rolled around in the collapsible play yard on the floor at Sarah's feet, making her cute little noises, staring up at a mobile of butterflies, birds and airplanes, happily gumming a series of rattles and rubber toys.

Logan checked in every two or three hours in case Sarah had questions. If Sophia was awake, he would spend a few minutes bent over the carrier or the play yard. The little girl made her goo-goo sounds at him and he answered each one with, "You're right" or "I agree completely" or "Yes, your mama is looking even more beautiful than usual today."

Sarah pretended to ignore him whenever he kidded

around with Sophia. She focused on her laptop, her slim fingers working the mouse, swiftly tapping the keys. But Logan didn't miss the slight flush to her cheeks or the smiles she tried so hard to hide.

If Sophia was fussy, he would pick her up and walk her around the office a little until she quieted. The first time that happened, Sarah said, "You don't have to hold her. She's fine, really. I usually wait a few minutes before I rush to calm her. Half the time, she settles down by herself."

He stroked the baby's wispy hair and kept walking back and forth. "Are you saying you don't *want* me to pick her up?"

"Of course not. You're sweet to do it. Hey, knock yourself out."

"Thanks." He grinned at the baby and she grinned right back. "Because Sophia and I, we have a good thing going on."

Sarah kept right on typing. "She has you wrapped around her teeny-tiny finger is what you mean."

"Exactly," he answered proudly. "And Sophia and I, we like it that way."

Once he'd had a little quality time with Sophia, Logan would answer any questions that Sarah had for him and then leave her to her work. It wasn't easy, keeping his visits to the office at a minimum and his hands to himself. Every time he went in there, he longed to move in behind her, bend close, breathe in the scent of her, maybe turn her chair around and steal a steamy kiss. But he needed to show her that he was capable of respecting her workspace.

By Friday afternoon, though, he was anticipating the coming evening like crazy.

He hoped that she was, too.

There was a white van parked at the curb in front of her Pine Street cottage when Sarah answered the door at seven Friday evening with Sophia in her arms.

"Cute house," said Logan, looking way too hot in dress jeans, a snow-white shirt and a leather jacket that probably cost more than a Ford Fiesta.

She saw over his shoulder that his fancy crew cab pickup was right behind the van—the van that had "Giordano's Catering for All Occasions" printed in flowing red script across the side. He was having dinner catered? That wasn't the deal. She was about to question him when Sophia seemed to recognize him.

The baby pulled her fist from her mouth and giggled out a nonsense word, "Adaduh," as her face lit up in a giant, toothless smile. Before Sarah could stop her, she swayed toward him, fat arms outstretched.

"Whoa," he said. "Okay." And he caught her neatly on one arm. "I've got you."

"Gack!" She patted his face with her little hand.

"She'll get drool on your jacket," Sarah warned.

"I don't care." He made a silly face at Sophia, who giggled in delight and patted his cheek some more.

A dark-haired woman emerged from the passenger side of the van and bustled up the front walk as the driver got out, went around and opened the van's rear doors.

"This is a lot more than takeout," Sarah chided.

"It'th better than takeout," he said with a lisp because

he was gumming Sophia's fingers. He caught the baby's hand and kissed her tiny fingertips. Sophia chortled as he suggested, "Wait and see."

Really, the guy was impossible.

The caterer introduced herself. "I'm Mia." The burly driver came up the steps behind her. "This is Dan." She asked where Sarah wanted them to set up.

Sarah led Mia and Dan into the dining alcove. "How can I help?" she asked.

Logan took her arm and pulled her over next to him. "Step back and let them work."

Mia and Dan swiftly set the table with white linen, fancy china, real silver and shining glassware. There were candles—tall, white ones in silver candlesticks. It was really beautiful.

Logan still held Sophia. The baby waved her arms and jabbered away as Mia and her assistant took the food into the kitchen. They put the salads and dessert in the fridge and set the rest out on the counter in chafing dishes to keep it warm.

"We'll serve ourselves," Logan said when the caterers were finished setting up.

Mia explained that she would be by around eleven the next morning to collect the dishes and everything else. "Just leave it all on the porch if you're not going to be here or if you plan to sleep late." She and her helper headed out the door. Sarah followed, thanked them again, and stood there in the doorway as the van started up and drove away.

She turned back to the man and the baby. He'd given Sophia the rubber frog Sarah had left on the coffee table. Sophia chewed on it contentedly, resting her head against his broad chest.

"You shouldn't have," said Sarah flatly.

"You love it," he replied.

And yeah, she kind of did.

Logan was getting downright attached to Sophia. She seemed to really like him, too. Yeah, she got drool on his jacket, but so what? She chewed on her rubber frog and occasionally glanced up at him. "Ack," she would say, or "Bah," like she was telling him something really important.

She was wearing pajamas, white ones with pink sheep printed on them, all ready for bed. Sarah said no way was she sitting down to that beautiful dinner while the baby was still awake.

When Sophia started to get fussy, Sarah took her. "You can hang your jacket on that rack by the door," she said, as she knelt to put the baby on a play mat on the living room floor, setting a mobile over her with little forest animals hanging from it. Sophia didn't even try to turn over as she often did when Sarah had her in the play yard at the ranch. She just gummed her frog and stared up at the slowly rotating bears and squirrels.

Logan caught Sarah's hand as she rose from the floor. He turned her around so they were facing each other. Back at the ranch earlier that day, she'd been wearing dress jeans and a pale green button-up. Now, she wore a silky bronze-colored shirt with a nice low neckline that clung to the rounded curves of her breasts. "I like this shirt." He liked her snug jeans, too, which were a little darker brown than the shirt. On her feet she wore flats in a leopard print.

"Thank you." She smiled at him. Slowly. All he wanted was to kiss her.

Somehow, he controlled himself. "You should give me a tour."

She pointed at the short hall a few feet away. "Two bedrooms and a bath through there." And she gestured past the dining area. "Kitchen through that arch there. It's small, but it's home." She gave a wry grin, a grin that enticed him because everything about her enticed him.

And he couldn't resist a moment longer. He reeled her in, caught her face between his hands and kissed her. She tasted so good and she kissed him back, shyly at first and then more deeply.

The feel of her against him was temptation personified. He wanted to take it further. But now was hardly the moment, with their dinner still uneaten and her baby staring up at them from the floor.

Reluctantly, he broke the kiss and pressed his forehead to hers. "I could get used to this."

She pulled back. He caught her fingers before she could fully escape him. They stood in the middle of her small living room, holding hands, regarding each other. "You're a very determined guy, Logan."

"You noticed, huh?"

She did that thing, catching her lower lip between her teeth. He loved when she did that. It also drove him just a little bit wild. He ached to bite that lip for her.

"You're here in my house," she said. "My baby has a crush on you. I don't believe this is happening. This is everything I promised myself I wasn't going to do again."

"It's just dinner," he reminded her—though it was a whole lot more than that. And both of them knew it.

But he would tell whatever little white lies he had to tell to get closer to her.

She glanced down at Sophia. He followed her gaze. The baby lay, her arms above her head, rubber frog abandoned, sound asleep, as the mobile of forest animals continued to turn slowly over her head.

"I'll just put her in her crib," Sarah whispered, easing her fingers from his grip and kneeling to gather the little girl into her arms. Sophia's tiny mouth stretched wide in a yawn, but she didn't open her eyes.

Sarah carried the baby down the short hall and Logan followed. She entered the room on the right. He remained in the open doorway as she laid Sophia in her crib and settled a light blanket over her.

When she turned and saw him standing there, he felt a little guilty for trailing after her. He was constantly pushing the boundaries with her and he knew he had to be careful not to go too far. Sarah just might send him packing.

But apparently, the sight of him in the doorway to her baby's bedroom didn't bother her. Those golden eyes were soft and accepting of his presence there.

She came to him. "Let's have dinner," she whispered. "I'm starving."

Sarah dished up the food as Logan lit the candles and opened the bottle of Chianti he'd ordered to go with the meal.

They sat down to eat. It was heaven, Sarah thought, even if it was exactly the kind of intimate evening she should never have let happen.

But still...

A beautiful meal and a nice glass of wine, a gorgeous man across the table from her. It really was a special treat. She hadn't had a single sip of anything with alcohol in it since the day the home pregnancy test came out positive. Not only was drinking bad for the baby, who had time for it? Not Sarah.

However, she'd stopped nursing two months ago. The stress in Chicago had been killing her and it was just too much, all that pumping to get enough milk for when Sophia was at day care. Sarah had given up the fight and switched to formula. It wasn't as good for her baby—or her wallet—but at least Sophia seemed to be doing fine on a bottle. She was even starting to eat pureed foods.

And if Sarah had a glass of wine or two tonight, her baby wouldn't suffer for it.

"Hey," said the killer-handsome guy across the table.

"Hmm?"

"You're frowning. Something wrong with the wine?"

"No way." She raised her glass to him. "It's delicious. And the veal is amazing."

He seemed pleased. "Told you so."

The conversation flowed easily. They talked about her progress on the Ambling A accounts. Logan reported that his second-born brother, Hunter, and his six-year-old daughter, Wren, had moved into one of the three cottages on the property. Knox, fifth in the birth order, had claimed a second cottage. Finn and Wilder had taken rooms in the main house with Max, Logan and Xander.

"Six of you boys and Max, too," Sarah teased. "That's a lot of testosterone."

"We get along," he said. "Mostly. Dad can drive us all kind of crazy, but his heart's in the right place."

Was it? She didn't know what to think about Max. "If you say so. How did your brothers react to the news that Max has offered Viv and Caroline a million bucks to find you guys brides?"

He laughed. "They're used to his wild ideas and schemes. Mostly, we all told him to knock it off, that we could find our own brides when we were damn good and ready. But Dad won't give up. He's relentless when he's got a plan and more often than not, he makes his plans come together, no matter how out-there they might seem at first."

What was he telling her, exactly? She shouldn't even let herself try to figure out what he meant. But she did wonder.

Would he be going out with the women Viv and Caroline introduced him to? Did he actually expect he would end up married to one of them? He certainly couldn't mean *her*. She wasn't marrying anyone, thank you very much. And Max had made it more than clear that he didn't want Logan getting too close with the single mom from Falls Mountain Accounting.

Not that Logan seemed like the kind of guy who did things his father's way. And the simple fact that he was here, sitting across from her over this perfect meal he'd arranged, well, that said something, didn't it? He really did seem to like her and her little girl, too.

And what about those amazing kisses they'd shared—the ones she probably shouldn't have let happen? Was he going to go from kissing her so thrillingly to taking some other girl out next Friday night?

He gazed across the table at her, those superfine blue eyes full of humor—and other things, sexy things she also wasn't going to think about.

She held out her wineglass and he filled it again. "So, tell me about your life in Seattle."

He said he'd gone to the University of Washington and teamed up with college friends to start investing in real estate. The business had grown. He'd scored big with some large commercial properties. "I loved it," he said. "There's always something going on in Seattle. The nightlife is great and the work kept me interested. But I missed the wide-open spaces, I guess you could say."

"Any serious relationships?" she asked. Because why not? She wanted to know. And after her TMI crying jag at the ranch the other day, she figured she deserved to hear at least a little about his past loves.

"None," he said.

She laughed. "Did you really have to go into so much detail?"

He lifted one hard shoulder in a half shrug. "Okay, I've dated exclusively a few times. But I've never been married or engaged, never even lived with a woman."

She turned her wineglass slowly by the stem. "So, you're a player?"

"Smile when you say that."

She raised the wine to her lips and savored its rich

taste of earth and dark cherries. "Looks like Viv and Caroline will have their work cut out for them with you."

He gazed at her way too steadily. The look in his eyes caused a warm shiver to slide over her skin. "There's only one girl I'm interested in and I think you know that. I want to be with *you*, Sarah, and I'm hoping that you'll realize you like being with me, too."

She did realize it. She realized the hell out of it and that didn't ease her mind one bit—and what was she doing right now?

Exactly what she *shouldn't* be doing, staring at his mouth. Staring at those lips of his and remembering the delicious pleasure of his kiss.

Blinking, she refocused. Somehow, this meal seemed to be turning into a seduction. She couldn't allow that.

But the food was so good and the man across from her so very charming. Plus, as usual, she was exhausted. The delicious wine seemed to be going straight to her head, making her body feel loose and easy, giving everything a sort of hazy glow.

He asked her about the brushstrokes of different-colored paint on the wall next to the dining-room hutch and in the kitchen and the hallway and the baby's room, too.

She explained that she had plans to paint the cottage, to make it bright and cheery and really hers. "Unfortunately," she admitted with a resigned sigh, "painting my new place is low priority right now. Too many other things come first."

"Like?"

"Making a living and taking care of my baby. I've

got a million things to do if I ever get a free minute. Starting with sleeping. That would be a thrill."

When their plates were empty, Logan granted her a slow smile full of sexy devilment. "Ready for dessert?"

He insisted on serving her. It was chocolate semifreddo, essentially a frozen mousse. And it was amazing. She ate it slowly, savoring every bite, trying to keep her moans of sheer delight to a minimum.

When she was done, Logan pushed back his chair. "I'll clean up and put everything out on the porch, all ready for Mia and Dan to pick up in the morning." He came to her side of the table and held out a hand to her.

She stared at that offered hand, a shiver of awareness warming her skin to have him so close. "Oh, no," she said.

"Oh, no what?"

She shifted her gaze up, into his waiting eyes. Really, she felt so good, easy and lazy with the wine and the wonderful food—and what was it she'd been about to say? She blinked and remembered. "You sit back down. I'll do it."

"Give me your hand." When she hesitated, he took it anyway and pulled her to her feet.

"Logan, seriously," she protested. "You provided this amazing dinner. The least I can do is clear the table."

"Uh-uh." He took her by the shoulders and turned her around. "Start walking."

"No, really, I—"

"Straight ahead." He guided her to the living room sofa, turned her around a second time and then gently pushed her down. "Relax. I've got this." He seemed determined.

And she *was* relaxed—more than relaxed. She felt downright lazy. "Go ahead." She waved him away. "Do all the work."

He bent close and pressed his lips to her forehead. "I will."

She watched him stride back to the table, admiring the width of his shoulders and his truly stellar behind. Really, did he have to be so good-looking both coming and going?

"Not fair," she muttered as her eyelids kept trying to droop shut and her body sagged against the armrest. She grabbed the throw pillow and stuck it under her head.

What could it hurt to shut her eyes? Not for long, of course. Just for a minute…

Chapter Four

Twenty minutes later, Logan had the table cleared, the leftovers transferred to plastic containers and stored in the fridge and everything else stacked and waiting on the front porch, ready for pickup the next day.

By then, Sarah was completely conked out on the sofa, looking so cute, with her head on a pillow, her lips softly parted, her feet still on the floor.

She stirred when he knelt to slide off her shoes. "Wha…? Logan?"

"Shh," he soothed her. "It's okay," he whispered. "Close your eyes."

"Hmm…" And she drifted back to dreamland again. He eased her feet up onto the cushions, settled the sofa blanket over her and placed a chaste kiss at her temple.

Should he grab his jacket and let himself quietly out the door?

Probably.

But what fun was that?

He took the easy chair across from the sofa, hooked one booted foot across the other knee and settled in to watch her sleeping.

What was it about her? he asked himself for the umpteenth time. He liked her. Too much? Maybe. But she had grit. He admired that. She was beautiful and smart with a wry sense of humor. And every time he kissed her, he wanted more.

More of the taste of those sweet lips of hers. More of her laughter and more of her sighs. More of all of her.

It surprised him, his own patience in this never-quite-happening seduction of her that he'd been knocking himself out to orchestrate—so far to minimal success.

There was just something about her. She gave him... *feelings*, which was emo and weird for him. But good. Somehow, it didn't bother him at all, having feelings for Sarah. She was so independent and determined, but so womanly, too. She tried to be tough, but she had a tender heart. He could sit here across from her in the easy chair all night, watching her sleep, wanting to sketch her.

Logan had always been good at drawing things. Give him a tablet full of paper and a pen or a pencil and he could spend hours doodling pictures of trees, houses, horses—you name it.

Early on, he'd discovered that women loved a cowboy with a little artistic talent. In high school and later, at UW, he would carry a sketchpad wherever he went. If he saw a woman he admired, he would draw a picture of her, which would get her attention and also bring other women flocking around him. If guys ribbed him about being an artsy-fartsy type, he would just shrug and say it worked great with the girls.

Nobody needed to know it went deeper. Drawing pictures of the things and the people around him focused him somehow, brought him a sense of peace within himself.

And he'd just happened to notice that Sarah had a small desk tucked into a corner of her kitchen. Would she be pissed at him if he looked in there for some paper and a pencil?

He got up to check and found just what he was looking for: a large spiral-bound notebook of unlined white paper. She also had several #2 pencils in the pen drawer, all of them sharpened to perfect points. No surprise there. He could have guessed that Sarah was a woman who kept her pencils sharp. He took two, just in case he broke the lead on one.

Back in the easy chair, he got down to it, quickly sketching his favorite accountant as she snoozed on the couch. He finished a first attempt of her, head-to-toe, her hands tucked under her chin on the pillow, the bottom half of her covered in the brown-and-white couch blanket that looked good with her hair and that silky shirt she was wearing. He could almost wish he had colored pencils or pastels to capture the colors of her, too.

He'd just started on a close-up of her face when whiny sounds erupted from the baby monitor on the hutch in the dining alcove.

"Ahduh. Unh. Ga?" Sophia was awake and if he didn't do something, Sarah would be, too.

Pencil and notebook still in hand, he scooped up the monitor as he passed it.

The door to the baby's room was shut. He pushed it open. Enough light bled in from the living room for him to see that she'd kicked off her blanket and grabbed hold of her own toes.

"Maaa?" She'd turned her head to look at him through the slats of her crib.

Laughing a little at the sight of her with her little hands clutching her feet, he switched on the table lamp and shut the door to mute the noises she was making.

"Duh," she said. "Uh?"

He dropped the pencil and notebook by the lamp, turned off the monitor and put it down on top of the pad.

Sophia let go of her feet and fisted her hands. She made a sound that was more of a cry than a nonsense word.

He went to her and scooped her up. "Hey. Hey, it's okay."

Her lower lip was quivering. And then she did start to cry. She smelled like a dirty diaper, which was probably the problem. It couldn't be that complicated to clean her up, could it?

The dresser a few feet from the crib had a pad on top and shelves above with stacks of diapers and wipes.

He could do this.

Sophia chewed on her hand and looked at him through big, blue tear-wet eyes.

"It's okay. We got this," he promised her as he laid

her down on the pad with its soft cotton cover printed with ladybugs and smiling green caterpillars.

Actually, it wasn't that difficult. Everything he needed was right there within reach. Sophia whimpered softly up at him as he worked, watching his every move as though she couldn't quite trust him to know what he was doing.

He couldn't blame her for having her doubts. His experience with babies was nil. When Hunter's little girl, Wren, was born, Logan had been busy making his mark in Seattle real estate. Yeah, he'd gone home to Texas maybe twice while his niece was still a baby. He'd done the classic uncle things—shaking a rattle over her crib, holding her while someone snapped a picture. That was it. Diaper changing never once came into play.

But he managed it with Sophia well enough. By the time he got her back into her pajamas, she'd stopped fussing.

He took her in his arms. "What'd I tell you? Stick with me, kid. Ready to go back to bed now?"

"Unh." Her lip started quivering all over again.

Sixty seconds later, she was making soft bleating sounds—not a full-out cry, but he had zero doubt she would get there if he didn't figure out what she needed very soon. He paced the small room, patting her back, trying to soothe her.

Maybe she was hungry.

He hated to open the door. Her cries were bound to wake Sarah—which would be good, wouldn't it?

Hell, yeah. Sarah would know what to do.

But she'd been sleeping so peacefully when he left

her. And she really could use a little rest. He didn't want to disturb her unless there was no other choice.

Advice from an expert. That was what he needed. Wren's mom had died shortly after her birth, leaving Hunter to raise his daughter on his own. Hunter had been a hands-on kind of dad.

As Logan paced the floor and did his best to soothe the baby, he dug his phone from his pocket and attempted to text his brother, which turned out to be a losing game with Sophia squirming in his arms.

He gave in and punched the call button.

Hunter answered on the first ring. "Logan. What?" By then, Sophia was steadily fussing. "Is that a baby? What are you doing with a baby?"

Logan continued to pace the floor and pat the baby as he briefly explained that Sarah was sleeping and he didn't want Sophia to wake her.

"Sarah. Sarah Turner, you mean? The woman you hired to set up the ranch accounts?"

"Right."

"You've got a thing going on with the accountant? Fast work, big brother."

"Hunter, focus. I need some help here. I changed Sophia's diaper, but she's still not settling down."

"You, of all people. Falling for the bean-counting single mom." Hunter chuckled.

"Think you're pretty funny, huh? The baby's crying and I need some help here."

Hunter got serious. "She could be sleepy."

"She *was* sleeping. She woke up."

"Uh, right. How old is she, exactly?"

"Who? Sarah?"

"The baby."

"Five months?"

"What? You're not sure?"

"I'm sure enough. Five months."

"Okay, so I see three options to start. Is she flushed and feverish?"

Sophia's cheeks were pink, but that could be from fussing. He felt her little forehead. "I don't think she has a fever."

"She's probably hungry, then. Or maybe teething." He said Logan should look in the freezer for a cold teething toy. As for something to eat, he should look for formula and follow the instructions on the packaging. "Or wait. Is Sarah nursing? I know zip about that. Wren was on formula from the first."

Was Sarah nursing? Logan didn't know, and that really bugged him. A guy should know if the woman he couldn't stop thinking about was nursing. Shouldn't he? "I've never seen her nurse the baby. But bottles. I've seen her feed Sophia with those."

"Are you in the kitchen? If there's formula, follow the directions on the packaging." Hunter added, almost to himself, "Or then again…"

Logan kept pacing, the phone tucked under his chin so he could use the hand that wasn't supporting the baby to stroke her back and hold her steady as she squirmed. He really didn't get what his brother was trying to tell him. "You're saying that I shouldn't look for formula, after all?"

"No. I was just thinking you could look for baby food, too. Sarah might be introducing her to solids at this point."

Sophia gave a loud cry that faded into a pained whine. She flopped her head down on Logan's shoulder with a sad little sigh.

"Logan? You okay?"

"Not exactly. If I go in the kitchen, Sarah will probably hear her fussing and wake up. The whole point is for Sarah *not* to wake up."

"Then put the baby in her crib and go to the kitchen without her."

"She's upset. I don't want to leave her alone."

"Yeah, I know. It's hard when they can't tell you what's bothering them. But I don't know what more to suggest. You've already changed her diaper and she doesn't have a fever. Your best bets are that she's hungry or teething."

"Gotcha. Gotta go."

Hunter was wishing him luck as Logan ended the call. He dropped the phone on top of the notebook next to the baby monitor. Then he carried Sophia back to her crib.

"I'm going to put you in your bed," he explained, as if she could understand actual words. "And then I will run and see what I can find to make you feel better. I'll be right back." He peeled her off his shoulder and gently laid her in the crib.

She let out a sharp cry and then a longer one, her little face scrunching up, her arms reaching for him.

"Right back. Promise." Before he could relent and pick her up again, he got out of there, shutting the door on Sophia's unhappy cries.

As he raced by the living room, he noted that at least

Sarah was still dead to the world. He really hoped he wouldn't end up having to wake her.

In the kitchen, he found powdered formula and some jars of pureed baby food in the cupboard. There were also a couple of plastic baby toys in the freezer. He decided to try the frozen toy pretzel first. Grabbing it, he rushed back to the baby's room, where Sophia was miserable, wailing now, her face scrunched up, beet red. He slid in and quickly shut the door behind him.

She continued to cry and he felt terrible. If the teething toy didn't work, he would have to get Sarah.

"It's okay. I'm here." Her crying stopped when he picked her up, but then started in again. "Come on. Try this." He touched the pretzel to her lips and a miracle happened. She took it in her mouth and even grabbed hold of it with her little hand.

A relieved sigh escaped her as she worked her gums on the frozen toy. She chewed the toy and regarded him so seriously, a last tear shining on her fat cheek, reminding him of her mother the other day, so sad over all the ways her life hadn't turned out as she'd planned.

He gently rubbed the tear away. "Feel better?"

"Unh."

"I'm going to take that as a yes."

He carried her over to the rocker in the corner and sat down. She gummed her pretzel and drooled on his shirt as he rocked her gently.

Eventually, she let go of the pretzel. It fell to his lap. That was when he realized she'd gone back to sleep.

He just sat there rocking her for a while longer because really, she was just the cutest thing, smacking her lips now and then as she slept, yawning once or twice.

When he finally got up and tucked her back in her crib, she didn't even stir.

Before he turned off the lamp, he grabbed the spiral-bound notebook he'd stolen from the kitchen desk and dashed off a few sketches of her all cozy and peaceful, looking like a little angel as she slept.

Sarah came awake slowly.

She was lying on the sofa with a blanket over her. The lamp in the corner, turned down low, cast a soft glow over the living room. Across the coffee table, in the easy chair, Logan snored softly, his drooping head braced on a hand. She sat up and squinted at the little clock on the side table.

It was after two in the morning. The baby monitor that had been on the hutch was now on the coffee table next to a plastic teething pretzel that she remembered putting in the freezer the afternoon before. The only reason she could think of for Logan to remove the toy from her freezer was to soothe Sophia's teething pain.

Also on the coffee table were a full-size notebook and two pencils, most likely from her desk in the kitchen. The open pad was turned away from her, the top pages turned back. He'd been drawing something, though from this angle, she couldn't see what.

Quietly, so as not to disturb him, she picked up the notebook and flipped through the pages.

There were eight drawings total, five of her and three of Sophia. Logan had been sketching pictures of her and her daughter as they slept. They were beautiful, those sketches. Who knew the guy had that sort of talent? She'd had no clue.

It felt a little strange to think of him watching her, drawing her without her knowledge. But it didn't bother her, not really. And that was strange in itself, that she didn't mind he'd done the sketches without her knowledge. She wasn't really that trusting of a person, especially when it came to Sophia. She had a hard time counting on anyone but herself. Yet she'd dropped right off to sleep last night and left him to take care of Sophia. She did trust him, at least a little. And she loved the drawings.

She wanted them—especially the ones of her little girl. Maybe if she asked him nicely, he would give them to her.

And maybe she was growing kind of attached to him already. *Fond* of him, even. On top of being so strongly attracted to him.

Not good. Not wise at all.

But right now, she was too tired to ponder where this thing between her and the gorgeous, surprisingly artistic, baby-soothing man sleeping in her easy chair might be going. She got up, covered him with the blanket, grabbed the baby monitor, switched off the lamp and headed for her bed.

Sarah woke to daylight, feeling more rested than she had in months.

She blinked in surprise when she saw the time. Past eight. Sophia often slept through the night lately, but never as late as eight in the morning.

The monitor by the bed was silent, the screen dark. She touched it and it lit up with an image of Sophia's empty crib.

Sarah's heart started racing with the beginnings of alarm—until she remembered the baby-soothing rancher she'd left sleeping in her easy chair last night.

As soon as she opened her bedroom door, she heard Logan's low laughter and her baby's happy cooing. She followed the sounds into the kitchen where he sat at the two-seater table with Sophia on his lap. He fed her baby cereal as she waved her arms and babbled out nonsense syllables.

A messy business, feeding Sophia.

Sarah leaned in the arch to the dining alcove. "I would bet you that more cereal has ended up on you and the baby than in her mouth."

With the back of his hand, he wiped a dab of the stuff off his beard-scruffy cheek. "I never take a bet I know I'll lose." And then his gaze wandered over her, down the length of her body and back to meet her waiting eyes again.

Her hair was a mess. She wore her old robe over sleep shorts and a T-shirt with a frayed neckline. And yet somehow, that lingering glance of his made her feel like the prettiest girl in Rust Creek Falls.

"Sleep well?" His voice was low and deliciously rough.

"I did, yeah." She must have gotten a good ten hours total. Because of him. "Thank you."

"Anytime." And he smiled at her.

She felt that smile of his as an explosion of warmth in the center of her chest.

Oh, this guy was dangerous. She could so easily get in over her head with him.

"Bacon and eggs?" she asked.

"I would love some."

A half hour later, he reluctantly headed for the door. She thanked him again for the beautiful evening and the priceless hours of glorious sleep.

"I'll call you," he promised as she ushered him out. She made a noncommittal noise in response and quickly shut the door.

In the living room, the pictures he'd drawn were still there on the coffee table. Apparently, he didn't want them. Which was great. Because she did. She would find frames for the ones of Sophia. And the ones of her, well, she would keep them as a reminder of him. Because he was a great guy and last night had been lovely.

But it was just too risky to go there. Her life now at least had a certain equilibrium. She couldn't afford to take chances with her heart.

He texted her that afternoon. I had a long talk with Sophia last night. She finally opened up to me and admitted that she wants us to spend more together.

Even feeling edgy and sad that she had to call a halt with him, she couldn't help smiling. Right. Sophia's a big talker. Too bad she doesn't use actual words yet.

I understand her. We communicate, Sophia and I. How about tonight? I'm supposed to go to this family thing. Come with me. Or if you want to go somewhere just the two of us, that's even better. I know a steak house in Kalispell. You're going to love it.

Her hopeless heart filled with longing—to spend another great evening with him. But that had to stop. Lucky for her, she already had a date with Lily for tonight. Sorry, I can't. It's a girls' night. Just my friend Lily and me.

Damn. Sunday? Come out to the ranch? Or maybe a picnic in Rust Creek Falls Park? Sophia would love it.

No, really. I can't. I'll see you Monday at the ranch. I still have a couple more days' work getting everything set up.

He didn't respond right away. But then, an hour later, her phone rang. She saw it was him and tried to hold strong, to let it go to voice mail. They could talk about it Monday. She could explain that it wasn't going to work, that she couldn't go out with him anymore.

But having it out with him Monday wouldn't be right, would it? She was going to the Ambling A to work. She needed to keep personal discussions out of the work environment.

Really, it had to be done now. She answered on the third ring. "Hi."

"What's going on, Sarah?" His voice was so careful. Flat. Controlled.

She needed to just do it. Get it over with. Move on. "I really can't do this, Logan. I can't go out with you again—I mean, I *won't* go out with you again. You're a wonderful man and I really like you, but it's not going to happen between us."

Dead silence from his end.

"Logan? Are you still there?"

"Yeah. And all right. I hear you. I'll see you Monday—and don't worry. You want it strictly business, so I'll give you what you want."

Chapter Five

Sarah's mom arrived right on time that night. She took Sophia into her arms and followed Sarah into the kitchen and then the baby's room as Sarah explained what to feed her, when to put her to bed and how the baby monitor worked.

"Amazing," declared her mother, thoroughly impressed. "Nowadays a baby monitor is a mini-security system. And the picture is so clear, honey."

Sarah still had trouble reconciling this pretty, confident, enthusiastic woman with the quiet, dutiful mouse of a mother who had raised her. "Yeah, well. As you can see, it's pretty simple. You shouldn't have any trouble with it."

Flo blew a gentle raspberry against Sophia's cheek and the baby giggled. Sarah watched them. Never in her life had she expected to see her mom blow a raspberry. It was all too strange and hard to believe.

"How's my girl?" Flo asked the baby.

Sophia giggled again and added, "Bah. Ga."

Sarah kind of tuned them out. She kept thinking about Logan, feeling heartsick about cutting things off with him.

She knew it was for the best.

But why did it have to hurt so much?

She'd only had the one evening with him. How could she have gotten so attached so fast?

"You seem kind of down, sweetheart. What's bothering you?" Flo asked as Sophia chortled in glee and bounced up and down in her grandma's arms. "Could this have anything to do with the fancy pickup that was parked in front of your house overnight last night?"

"Who told you that?"

"Honey, this isn't Chicago—it's Rust Creek Falls," her mom said as if that explained everything. And really, it kind of did.

In Rust Creek Falls, everybody pretty much knew everything about everyone else. They shared what they knew because they cared about their neighbors and also because it was a form of local entertainment to speculate about who was doing what—and with whom.

Sarah's mom regarded her with understanding, inviting her to share. And she really *wanted* to share…

But no. Uh-uh. Not happening. Bad idea.

It was over with Logan. Over without ever having really gotten started. There was nothing to talk about.

"Burdens are lighter when you share them," Flo advised with a radiant smile.

Say something. Anything. Just not about Logan.

"Actually, I, um, have noticed how well you and Dad seem to be getting along lately." Talk about an understatement. Sheesh. "And I've been kind of wondering what's happened between you two?"

She had been wondering, though she'd never planned to actually go there. Right now, though, even hearing about her parents' sex life would be preferable to discussing the man who'd become way too important to her way too fast.

"Oh, honey," said Flo. "I was beginning to think you'd never ask."

Beaming with pleasure, Sarah's mom told all. It had started with a routine visit to her new gynecologist and a pelvic exam that had led to a simple procedure that had changed everything for Flo and Mack.

"You see," said Flo, "as it turns out, I didn't heal properly after your birth, but I never realized that was the problem. It was just so painful to be intimate. And your father and I were hardly experienced. There was just that one time. Prom night. We got a little carried away. It was the first time for both of us.

"After that, we swore to wait. And then we learned you were coming and we got married earlier than we'd planned. We were just a couple of kids. What did we know? You arrived and your father went off to college. The next time we tried, well, it was awful for me. And no fun for him. We gave up, stopped trying—for years and years. Looking back, I can't believe we didn't at least try to figure out what might be wrong. But that's all changed now and I can't even describe how wonderful it is…"

There was more. Lots more. Stuff Sarah so didn't

need to hear. Some of it was kind of nice, though, about how her mom and dad had gotten counseling to increase their intimacy emotionally, too.

Eventually, when she'd heard way more than enough, she put up a hand. "So what you're saying is that you're happy together now, you and Dad?"

"Oh, sweetheart. Words cannot express."

"I'm glad, Mom." And she *was* happy for her parents. Plus, she'd managed to keep her mouth shut about Logan. "And look at the time! I really should get going."

"Have fun, darling. Say hi to Lily for me."

"Thanks, Mom. I will." Sarah kissed her baby and got out of there.

Maverick Manor had been built back in the eighties as a private home. Perched on a rise of land back from the highway, it was a giant log structure, one that had been enlarged even more when it became a hotel. Surrounded by manicured grounds, the place was rustic and luxurious at once. In the lobby with its vaulted, beamed ceiling, a giant mural depicted the early history of Rust Creek Falls and the pioneer families who had founded it.

When the hostess ushered Sarah into the dining room, Lily Hunt was waiting at a quiet corner table. They ordered their meal and a glass of house wine each.

Wine two nights in a row, Sarah thought. She was living the wild life, no doubt about it.

She studied her friend across the small table. Lily had striking red hair and gorgeous green eyes, yet most people in town considered her plain. She rarely wore makeup and kept her beautiful hair pulled smoothly back and anchored low at her nape. Some called her shy, but she wasn't, not really. Not with Sarah, anyway.

Once the waitress had served them their food, Lily said, "You mentioned the other day that you were working out at the Ambling A, setting up the books for Max Crawford and his sons..."

Sarah guessed where her friend was going. "You heard about the deal Max made with Viv and Caroline to find brides for Max's sons, didn't you?"

"Yep." Lily's smile bloomed slowly. "Me and everybody else in town."

"Why am I not the least surprised?"

Lily buttered her bread. "I also heard that Logan Crawford is completely smitten with a certain brilliant accountant, a beautiful single mom with an adorable little girl."

"Brilliant *and* beautiful, huh? You're flattering me. Why?"

"I only speak the truth." Lily was all innocence.

Sarah savored a bite of her petite filet and said nothing.

Lily leaned closer. "Tell me everything." Her green eyes gleamed with eager interest. "Hold nothing back."

After all that had happened since Lily babysat for her last Wednesday, Sarah could no longer pretend that nothing was going on between her and Logan.

She laid it all out. From her powerful attraction to Logan to Max's opposition to her as a possible match for his oldest son, to Logan's unflagging pursuit of her and their first "date" the night before.

"Logan's been nothing but wonderful," Sarah reported glumly. She explained that she'd ended it with him when he called that afternoon.

"I don't get it." Lily frowned. "Logan Crawford provides a sit-down catered dinner with all the trimmings, thrills you when he kisses you, takes care of Sophia both night and morning so you can get what you need the most—a good night's sleep. The man draws beautiful pictures of you and your baby. He doesn't leave you hanging but instead calls the next day to ask you out again. And yet you've decided it can't possibly work?"

Sarah loved Lily. But sometimes her friend was just way too logical. "I told you I've had it up to here with men and all the trouble they cause."

"So stay away from the jerks and troublemakers. But, Sarah, when a good one comes along you need to give the guy a chance."

"He's in his thirties. He's never been married. Yes, he's a great guy. But he's not interested in anything long-lasting."

"He *told* you that?"

"No. I just know it. I, well, I *sense* it."

Lily tipped her head to the side, frowning. "Suddenly, you're psychic?"

"Of course not. It's just that he told me he's never even lived with anyone. I seriously doubt he's suddenly decided he wants to try marriage, that's all."

"Where to even start with you? So he's in his thirties? It's a prime age for a guy to finally find the right woman. He's mature enough to know what he really wants—and anyway, what about you? Do *you* want to get married?"

"Did I say that? No, Lily. I don't want to get married. I'm not looking for a serious relationship. I honestly don't even want a date. I'm through with all that. I have Sophia and a job I'm good at and a cute little cottage that will be even cuter if I ever find the time and energy to fix it up a little."

"So then, be flexible."

Sarah slanted her friend a suspicious glance. "What, exactly, are you getting at?"

"Have a wonderful time with a terrific man for as long as it lasts. Because if you don't, Viv Dalton's dating service will be finding him someone who will."

Sarah sat up straighter. "That's okay with me."

"You don't mean that."

"Yes, I do." She tried really hard to tell herself that it wouldn't bother her in the least if Logan started seeing some other woman in town.

A murmur of voices rose from the far side of the big dining room.

Lily leaned in. "And speaking of the Crawford family…"

Sarah followed the direction of her friend's gaze and saw that the hostess was ushering in several new arrivals. They included Nate Crawford and his wife, Callie, a nurse at the local clinic. Nate's parents came in, too, as well as his pretty sister Natalie and his brothers and their wives.

And behind the local Crawfords came Max and six big men who looked a lot like him—including the tall, blue-eyed cowboy who made Sarah's heart beat faster and her cheeks feel much too warm. The Crawford clan took seats around a long table in the center of the room.

Lily whispered, "Max Crawford and sons, am I right?"

"How did you guess?" Sarah asked wryly.

"Everyone says they're all really good-looking." Her friend sipped more wine. "Everyone is right."

"Now that I think about it, Logan mentioned that there was some kind of family get-together tonight."

"A Crawford family reunion," said Lily. "Who's the cute little girl?" She gave a slight nod toward the blonde sprite who'd entered with Logan and his family.

"That would be Wren," said Sarah. "Her dad is Hunter Crawford. He's sitting to her left. Logan told me that Wren's mom died shortly after she was born."

"How sad." Lily was silent for a moment, kind of taking it all in. "Hmm…"

Sarah focused on her friend and tried really hard not to let her gaze stray to Logan. "Hmm, what?"

Lily tipped her head toward a table on the far side of the dining room. Viv and Caroline sat there, along with three other women who lived in town—single women, Sarah was reasonably sure. As Sarah watched, Viv turned in her chair and spoke to a woman at the next table over. Interestingly enough, that table was women-only, too.

Lily said, "Looks to me like Viv and Caroline's dating service is very much open for business."

Logan sat down at the table full of Crawfords, ordered a glass of eighteen-year-old Scotch and tried not to think about Sarah.

He noticed the wedding planners right away, as well as the pretty women at the table with them *and* at the next table over. Apparently, the wedding planners were already on the job providing potential brides for him and his brothers.

And his father, who had somehow ended up sitting next to him, was looking right at him. When Logan met Max's eyes, his dad winked at him. Logan gave his dad a flat stare—and then turned to face the other way.

Viv came over just to say hi. Max introduced her to Knox, Finn, Wilder and Hunter. She exchanged a few words with each of them, said hello to the local Crawfords and then rejoined the women.

Logan sat back and sipped his drink slowly as Nate Crawford explained how he and a few other movers and shakers in town had created Maverick Manor so that Rust Creek Falls would finally have a resort-style hotel.

When Nate finished his story, Finn, who was twenty-nine, fourth-born after Xander, got up and went over to where all the women sat. Viv introduced him to each of the women. He nodded and chatted them up a little before eventually wandering back to his seat. Wilder, last-born, rose a little later and strolled over to introduce himself, too. No way was Wilder ever going to let himself get tied down to one woman. But all the pretty ladies would have to find that out for themselves.

Logan's dad just couldn't leave it alone. As Wilder took his chair at the table again, Max leaned close and pitched his voice low for Logan's ears alone. "Yep. Lots of fine-looking women in this town. Take your pick, son. Viv will introduce you."

Logan didn't bother to answer. He just turned his head slowly and gave the old man another flat, bored stare.

Max got the message. He started yakking with Nate's dad, who was seated on his other side.

Logan was about to signal for a second Scotch when

he spotted Sarah and a red-haired woman sitting in a small, tucked-away corner of the dining room. He wasn't sure what made him turn halfway around in his chair and glance over there, but when he did, his eyes collided with hers.

She quickly looked away.

He should look away, too. But he didn't. Man, he had it bad. It hurt just to see her. And he was feeling sorry enough for himself at that moment to go ahead and indulge his pain by turning in his chair and staring.

Yeah, it was rude. But he didn't care.

Sarah wore a cream-colored sleeveless dress and her hair was down, soft and smooth on her shoulders. As he watched, the waitress appeared and set a check tray on the table between Sarah and her friend. The redhead whipped out her credit card. Sarah tried to argue, but it appeared that the redhead won. The waitress left to run the card. A few minutes later, she dropped off the tray again on her way to take an order at another table. The redhead signed the receipt and put her card away.

Any minute now, Sarah and her friend would get up and leave.

Today, she'd made it more than clear that she refused to get anything going with him. He needed to take a hint, order that second Scotch and let her go. He turned away.

And something inside him rebelled at the sheer wrongness of the two of them, so acutely aware of each other and trying so hard to pretend that they weren't.

Forget that noise. He couldn't let her go without at least saying hi.

Logan shoved back his chair.

Ignoring his dad's muttered, "Logan. Let it be," he pushed in his chair and turned for her table.

In three long strides, he was standing above her.

She put on a fake smile. "Logan, hi. This is my friend, Lily Hunt."

The redhead said, "Happy to meet you," and actually seemed to mean it. She got up. "I think it's time for me to go."

"Lily," Sarah protested. "Don't—"

Lily didn't let her finish. "Gotta go. Call me," she said and then she walked away.

Logan claimed the empty chair before Sarah could leap up and disappear.

"This is pointless," Sarah said—softly, in a tender, hopeful voice that belied her words. She had her hands folded together on the table.

When he put his palm over them, she didn't pull away.

In fact, she looked up at him, finally meeting his eyes.

Their gazes held.

The packed dining room and all the other people in it faded into the background. There was no one but the woman in the cream-colored dress sitting across the table from him, the connection he felt to her, the cool, smooth silk of her skin under his hand.

"How's Sophia?" he asked as he slipped his thumb in between her tightly clasped fingers.

A smile tried to pull at the corner of that tempting mouth. "Same as this morning. My mom's watching her."

"Does she miss me?"

A chuckle escaped her and a sweet flush stained her cheeks. "Stop…"

"You need to say that with more conviction—or not say it at all." He pretended to think about it. "Yeah. Say something like, 'Logan, I'm so glad you're here and I've changed my mind and would love to go out with you any time you say.'"

"I…"

"You…?" He succeeded in separating her hands and claimed one for himself, weaving their fingers together. They stared at each other across the table. Her fingers felt just right twined with his, and her cheeks had a beautiful, warm blush on them. He never wanted to let her go.

"Logan, I do like you. So much."

"Which is why you need to spend more time with me. And I don't mean as my accountant. I mean quality time. Personal time."

She drew in a slow, unsteady breath.

He knew then with absolute certainty that she was going to change her mind, tell him yes. Finally. At last.

Except that she was easing her hand free of his. "No. It can't go anywhere." She rose. "I meant what I said this afternoon. I would really appreciate it if you would please keep it business-only while I'm working for you at the ranch. And right now, I really do need to go."

Logan knew when he was beaten. She wasn't giving an inch and he needed to accept that. "All right. I'm through. See you Monday, Sarah. You can finish setting up the books. And that will be that."

With a tiny nod, she turned and walked away.

He rose and went back to join the family. The waitress brought him that second Scotch. He sipped it slowly and considered his options, of which there really was only one.

It was time to wise up, quit playing the fool. Sarah was never giving him a damn break and he needed to stop following her around like a lovesick calf.

A pretty blonde sitting with the other women at Viv Dalton's table gave him a friendly smile. He raised his glass to her and her smile got wider. She had dimples and big blue eyes.

What was that old song? *If you can't have the girl you want—want the girl you're with.*

Or something like that.

Chapter Six

The following Wednesday night, Logan took the blonde, whose name was Louise, out to that steak house he liked in Kalispell. Louise was a nice woman. As it turned out, she worked in Kalispell, teaching high school English. But she had her own little house in Rust Creek Falls inherited from a beloved aunt. She loved dancing, she said, especially line dancing.

Logan sat across from her and listened to her talk and wondered what it was about her.

Or more correctly, what it *wasn't* about her. She was pretty and friendly, intelligent and sweet. There was nothing *not* to like.

Except, well, he just didn't feel it. *Want the one you're with*, huh? Maybe. In some cases.

For him and Louise, though? Not so much.

Still, he nodded and smiled at her and tried to make all the right noises while his mind was filled with thoughts of Sarah.

She'd finished up at the ranch just that day. He wouldn't be seeing her again until tax time—except for now and then, the way people did in a small town. They would end up waving at each other as they passed on the street or maybe dropping by Buffalo Bart's Wings To Go at the same time.

"You're awfully quiet." Louise sent him another sweet, dimpled smile and sipped her white wine.

He was being a really bad date and he knew it. Sitting up a little straighter in his chair, he ordered his errant thoughts back to the here and now.

Later, when he took her home, Louise asked shyly, "Would you like to come in?"

He thanked her, said he had to be up before dawn and got the heck out of there.

Viv called him the next day. She said she'd talked to Louise, who'd reported that she really liked Logan but she just didn't feel that the "chemistry" was there. Logan had to agree.

He'd meant to tell Viv that he didn't need another date. But somehow, before he hung up, Viv had talked him into spending an evening with a girl named Genevieve Lawrence.

He and Genevieve met up on Friday night—in Kalispell again, at a cowboy bar she knew of. They danced and joked around. Genevieve knew ranch life and horses. She was a farrier by profession. They got along great, him and Genevieve.

But right away, Logan had that feeling, like she was

his sister or something. He could be best buds with Genevieve. But tangled sheets and hot nights with her to help him forget a certain amber-eyed accountant?

Never going to happen.

Plus, more than once between dances, Genevieve teased that he seemed like he was a million miles away.

And he kind of was. He was thinking of Sarah, and ordering himself to *stop* thinking of her. And then thinking of her anyway. Because dating other people didn't make him forget the woman he wanted. It just made him want her all the more.

At the end of that evening, Genevieve gave him a hug and whispered, "Whoever she is, don't be an idiot. Work it out with her."

It was great advice. Or it would have been, if only Sarah wanted to work it out with *him*.

When Viv called the next day, he explained that he really wasn't in the mood for dating. "So I won't be needing your, er, services anymore, thanks."

But evidently, Vivienne Dalton was downright determined to earn her million-dollar payout. Before he hung up, she'd convinced him to try a coffee date at Daisy's Donut Shop. "It's a half hour out of your life," promised Viv. "You get a coffee and a maple bar and if it goes nowhere, you're done."

Monday afternoon when Sarah dropped in at Falls Mountain Accounting, her mom was actually *not* behaving inappropriately behind the shut door of her father's office. Flo sat at her desk, her hair neatly combed, her shirt on straight. She was smiling, as she always did nowadays, typing away. The waiting area was empty.

"Hey, Mom."

Flo looked up from her desktop monitor with a welcoming smile. "Honey."

Sarah went on through to her own office and put the baby carrier, her backpack and laptop on her desk. In the carrier, Sophia was sleeping peacefully. Leaving the door open a crack so she would hear if the baby woke, Sarah returned to the main room, where her mom was now on the phone.

She picked up the stack of mail from the corner of Flo's desk and went through it, finding three envelopes addressed to her and setting the rest back down.

"Dad?" she asked as her mom hung up the phone.

Flo tipped her head toward Mack's shut door. "He's with a client."

"Okay, I'll be in my office if you—"

"Sweetheart." Her mom took off her black-framed reading glasses and dropped them on the desk. "I'm just going to ask."

Sarah had no idea what her mother could be getting at now. "Uh, sure. Ask."

"What went wrong between you and Logan Crawford?"

Just hearing his name hurt. Like a hard jab straight to the solar plexus.

"That face." Her mother made a circular gesture with her right hand, fingers spread wide. "That is not your happy face. Are you ever going to open up and talk to me?"

"I don't..." Her silly throat clutched and she hardswallowed. "I really don't want to talk about Logan."

"Oh, yes, you do. You're stubborn, that's all. You always have been. But here's what I know. A week ago last

Friday, Logan's pickup was parked in front of your house all night. Since then, well, *something* has gone wrong. The light has gone out of your eyes—don't argue. Your eyes are sad. They're full of woe. Then an hour ago, I drop by Daisy's for a cruller and a coffee and I see Logan sitting in the corner having donuts with some elegant-looking brunette. What *happened*, honey?"

"He was out with an elegant brunette?" God. That hurt so much—even though she knew very well she had no right at all to feel brokenhearted that he might be seeing someone else.

"Yes." Flo's tone had gentled. She gazed at Sarah with understanding now. "And yes, it was only coffee and a donut. I can't say beyond a shadow of a doubt that it absolutely was a date. But, well, sometimes a woman can just tell. You know?"

"No, Mom. I don't know."

"It's just that, the two of them together, well, there was a definite 'datish' feel about it."

"*Datish?* What does that even mean?"

"You *know* what I mean."

"I just said I didn't."

Flo waved her hand some more. "In any case, seeing your guy with another girl—"

"Mom, he is not my—"

"Yes, he is. If he wasn't your guy, you wouldn't be so crushed to learn that he had coffee with someone else." The phone rang.

"Aren't you going to get that?"

"Voice mail will get it. This is more important." They stared at each other through two more rings. As soon as the phone fell silent, Flo went right on. "Honey, I do understand your fears. You were always so sure of where you were going and how it would be for you. All your growing-up years, while your dad and I were stuck on a treadmill of unhappiness and emotional isolation, I just knew that for you, things would be different."

"You did?" Sarah felt misty-eyed that her mom had actually paid attention, had believed that Sarah would make a success of her life.

Flo nodded. "You had a plan and you were going to have it all—a high-powered job you loved, the right man at your side. And eventually, children to love and to cherish."

"Well, I do have Sophia, right? Things could be worse."

"But they could also be better, now, couldn't they? You haven't shared specific details with me, but here you are back at home, single with Sophia. It's patently obvious that things didn't work out according to your plan. You've been disappointed. Deeply so. But you can't just shut yourself off from your heart's desire because you've been let down a time or two. If you do that, you'll end up nothing short of dead inside. Take it from your mother who was dead inside herself for far too many years. Honey, you need to give that man a shot. If you don't, some other lucky girl is going to snap him right up."

That afternoon and through way too many hours of the night that followed, Sarah couldn't stop thinking about the things her mom had said.

In the morning, she had a nine o'clock appointment with a client out in the valley not all that far from the Ambling A. The meeting took a little over an hour.

When she finished, she secured Sophia's seat in the

back of her car, got in behind the wheel—and called Logan before she could think of all the reasons she shouldn't.

It rang twice. She was madly trying to decide whether to leave a message or just hang up when he answered. "Sarah?"

All he said was her name, but it was everything. Just to hear the slightly frantic edge to his always-smooth voice. As if he'd missed her. As if he was afraid she'd already hung up.

"Hey." Her mind went blank and her heart beat so fast she felt a little dizzy.

"Sarah." He said her name like it mattered. A whole lot.

And that gave her the courage to suggest a meeting. "I'm maybe five miles from the Ambling A and I was wondering if—"

"Yes. Meet me at the house. Come straight here."

She sucked in a deep breath and ordered her heart to slow the heck down. "Yeah?"

"I'll be waiting on the front porch."

Hope flaring in his chest and sweat running down his face, Logan stuck his phone back in his pocket. Luckily, he was within sprinting distance of the house.

"Gotta go." He jammed his pitchfork into the ground.

"What's up?" demanded Xander.

"Everything okay?" asked Hunter.

"Everything is great. Got a meeting with my favorite accountant," he called over his shoulder as he took off at a run, leaving Xander and Hunter staring after him, on their own to finish burning out the stopped-up ditch behind the main barn.

Entering the house through the back door, he hooked

his hat on a peg, toed off his dirty boots and then headed for the utility room, where he stripped off his shirt and used the deep sink there to wash away the smoke and grime.

Clean from the belt up, he raced upstairs to grab a fresh shirt and a pair of boots free of mud and cow dung. He was just stepping out the door, tucking his shirt in as he went, when Sarah's white Honda pulled up in front.

She got out before he could get there to open her door for her. God, she looked good in snug jeans, boots tooled with twining flowers and a white shirt, her thick hair swept up in the usual bouncing ponytail.

He skidded to a stop a foot away as she pulled open the back door and bent to unhook Sophia's seat.

"Here. Let me take her."

"Ga! Ba!" The baby waved both fat fists and smiled that gorgeous toothless smile at him as Sarah passed him the carrier.

"It's really good to see you, too," he said to Sophia.

"Pffffft," the little girl replied and then laughed that adorable baby laugh of hers.

Sarah anchored her baby pack on one shoulder. "I was wondering if we could talk?"

He almost had a heart attack from sheer gladness right then and there. "Absolutely. Let's go to the office."

In the office, Logan put Sophia's carrier on the desk.

Sarah dropped her pack beside the carrier, opened the front flap and pulled out a teething toy to keep the baby busy for a little while. She offered the toy and Sophia took it.

Pulse racing and a nervous knot in her stomach, hardly

knowing what she was going to say, Sarah turned to face the man she hadn't been able to stop thinking about.

How could such a hot guy just keep getting hotter? Surely that wasn't possible. Still, his eyes were bluer, even, than she remembered, his sexy mouth more tempting. His hair was wet, his shirt sticking to him a little, like he'd washed up quickly and hadn't really had time to dry himself off.

No doubt about it. He was, hands down, the best-looking man she'd ever seen. She wanted him so much. And she was so afraid it wouldn't work out.

But then he said, "Sarah," sweet and low and full of yearning.

The very same yearning she felt all through every part of her body.

And then he was reaching out. And she was reaching out.

She landed against his warm, hard chest with a tiny, hungry cry. His arms came around her and she tipped up her mouth to him.

His lips crashed down to meet hers. She sighed at that, at the perfection of being held by him, of having his mouth on hers. He smelled of soap and hay and something kind of smoky—and man. All man. So good. So right. So exactly what she needed.

She moaned low in her throat, her hands reaching, seeking, sliding over the hard, muscled planes of his chest and up to link around his neck.

He lifted his head, but only to slant that wonderful mouth the other way. His big hands roamed her back, pulling her closer, as though he could meld their two separate bodies into one.

And then from the doorway, a gravelly voice said, "Ahem. Hope I'm not interrupting."

With a gasp, Sarah broke the kiss.

She would have jumped back from Logan's embrace, except he didn't allow that. He cradled her close to him and said to his father, "Well, you *are* interrupting. Go away and close the door behind you."

"Aw, now." Max glanced down at his black boots and then up again with a rueful half smile. "I just need a minute or two."

"Whatever it is, it can wait."

"No, it can't. Come on, son. This won't take long."

Sarah felt awful and awkward and very unwelcome. It was disorienting—one minute swept away by the glory of a kiss and the next feeling somehow like an interloper in the Crawford house. "I should go."

Logan only held her tighter. "No way."

She couldn't stand this. Max in the doorway, refusing to leave them alone, Logan holding her too tightly, glaring at his dad.

"Really, Logan. Please. Let me go." She pushed more strongly at his chest and he finally released her.

Grabbing the baby carrier, she hitched the pack over her shoulder and turned for the door. Max stepped back. She swept past him and fled.

Max blocked the doorway again as soon as Sarah darted through it.

Logan barely held himself back from punching his own father right in the face. "Get out of my way, Dad."

Max didn't budge. "Now, son. You need to just let her go. She's not the one for you. She has a child and no man, which tells me things went bad with whoever that baby's daddy is. That's not a good sign. And beyond that, you never know. The father could show up any day now."

"You don't know what you're talking about. The father is out of the picture. Period. End of story."

"Well, whatever happened with the guy before you, I don't think I'm out of line in assuming it didn't end well. That means Sarah's been hurt and it won't be that easy to win her trust. I just don't get it. Why choose a woman with all that baggage? You're just asking for heartbreak."

Faintly, Logan heard the front door shut. "I don't know where you think you get off with this crap, but it's got to stop."

Max looked at him pleadingly. "Just give someone else a shot, that's all I'm saying."

"Pay attention, old man. Shut your mouth, open your eyes and use your ears for once. I've done it, let that wedding planner of yours set me up, gone out with the women she found for me. And you know what that's done for me? Not a thing—except to make me more certain that if there ever could be the one for me, Sarah's it."

"Now, that's not true."

"You're still not listening, Dad. It's a problem you have. Sarah is the one that I want. All your plotting and scheming isn't going to change that." Outside, he heard a car start up. He needed to go after her. "Move aside."

Max only braced his legs wide and folded his arms across his chest.

Fast losing patience, Logan made one more attempt to reason with the stubborn fool. "Okay. I get that whatever's eating you about Sarah is somehow related to what happened with Sheila way back when. You want to talk about that, fine, you talk about it. Just cut all the mystery and say right out what you're getting at. Because frankly, you're making no sense to me *or* to my brothers. For years, you've warned us off getting seriously involved with a woman. 'Have fun, boys,' you always said, 'but don't tie yourselves down.' And 'Marriage is like a walk in the park—Jurassic Park.'"

Max had the nerve to chuckle. "You have to admit, that was a good one."

"Not laughing." Logan glared at his father until Max's grin vanished. "What I want to know is why, out of the blue, you want all six of us married—just not with any woman who already has a child?"

"Think about it. It's not good for that baby, Logan. To get all attached to you and then to lose you. That's bad."

"Who says anyone's losing me?"

"You don't know what can happen."

"Nobody does. That's life. What I do know is that the way you just behaved with Sarah was rude. Unacceptable. Sarah's done nothing wrong and she's nothing like Sheila. Sarah would never turn her back on her own child the way Sheila did to us."

Max got the strangest look on his face. His straight shoulders slumped. All of a sudden, he looked every year of his age. "Maybe *I* did a few things wrong, too, you know? Maybe you and the other boys don't know the whole story of what happened with your mother."

"Maybe?" Logan got right up in his face over that one. "Dad, you are so far out of line, I don't know where to start with you."

"Son, I—"

"I'm not finished. If you haven't told us the whole story about Sheila, remedy that. Tell it. Do it now."

Max put up both hands and mumbled, "I'm only saying, if you really care about Sarah and her baby, you should do the right thing and walk away now."

"You're saying nothing and we both know it. And I am finished with listening to you tell me nothing. You keep that wedding planner off my back. You tell her I'm not going on any more dates with the women she's constantly calling to set me up with. I'm done dating women I don't want. I want Sarah. And right now, I'm going to do my level best to convince her to give me a real shot. Out of my way."

That time, Max didn't argue. He fell back and Logan headed for the door.

Outside, Logan found that Sarah's white CR-V was already long gone. At least he'd left his crew cab in front. He jumped in. Skidding and stirring up a mini-tornado's worth of dust, he headed for the highway.

He drove fast and recklessly all the way to town, not even knowing for sure if that was where she'd gone. It just seemed his best bet. If he didn't catch up with her, he would have to call her and he had a bad feeling that when he did, she wouldn't answer.

Damn the old man. This was all his fault. One minute, Logan had Sarah in his arms again and she was kissing him like she'd finally realized that she needed to give him a real, honest shot with her—and the next minute, his dad was there, acting like an ass, hinting of dark secrets, messing everything up.

If Max had ruined things for good with Sarah, there

was going to be big trouble as soon as Logan got back to the ranch.

He rolled into Rust Creek Falls on Sawmill Street and slowed down a little—after all, this was his town now. He didn't want to run any of his neighbors down. Plus, it would be hard reaching out to Sarah if the sheriff locked him up in jail. He rolled along at a sedate pace and then had to choose his first destination—her house on Pine or Falls Mountain Accounting on North Broomtail.

He slowed down at Pine—but he just had a feeling she'd gone to her office, so he rolled on by that turn, taking North Broomtail instead.

And he scored.

She was parked in front of her office, the back door open, bending to get Sophia's carrier out when he pulled his pickup in next to her.

Glancing back over her shoulder, she spotted him. Rising to her height, she turned. He jumped out and they faced off over the open car door.

"Sarah, I'm so sorry about my dad. You can't listen to—"

She put a finger to her lips and spoke softly. "Sophia's asleep."

He lowered the volume. "We need to talk. You know we do."

"Oh, Logan. I really don't—"

"*You* called *me*. You know you want to talk this through. Give me a break here. Don't change your mind. I missed you so damn much. Admit you missed me, too."

Her soft mouth hardened. "Yeah. Right. You missed me so much you were going out with someone else."

"Sarah…"

"Shh." She glanced up the street as a couple of older ladies came toward them on the sidewalk. They smiled and waved. He watched as Sarah forced her lips into an upward curve and waved back. Logan waved, too.

The ladies strolled on by, bending their heads close to speak in low voices, glancing more than once at Sarah and Logan.

Finally, the ladies moved on down the street and Sarah said, "Really, I don't—"

"I don't want anyone else," he vowed before she could finish telling him no all over again. "I only went out with those other women because you dumped me."

She scowled. "Dumped you? We had one date. You can't dump a person after just one date."

"Okay, so *dump* is the wrong word. You didn't dump me. You only said you didn't want to be with me and you wouldn't go out with me again. Fair enough?"

"I…" Her sleek brows drew together. "Wait a minute. Other *women*? There was more than just one?"

She hadn't known there were three dates?

He could punch his own face about now—trying so hard to explain himself and just making it worse. "Look. I was miserable. Viv Dalton kept calling. After the first one, I knew I wasn't interested and I told Viv I wasn't. But that woman is really determined and I was just sad, missing you, wanting you and trying to forget you. Those three dates did nothing for me. They didn't help me forget you. How could they when all I did was think about you?"

She was softening. He could see it in those golden-brown eyes, in the way she looked at him. Intense.

Reluctant—but expectant, too. "You, um, thought about me?"

"Only you. And I'm done. Finished with trying to forget you by wasting the time of nice women I'm not the least interested in."

"You are?"

"I am. I swear it to you—and I also promise that I'm not rushing you. I'm only hoping that maybe we could try again, take it slower, if you need it slower. Be…I don't know, be *friends*." He tried not to wince when he offered the friend zone. Being her friend wasn't going to satisfy him, no way. "Whatever you want. As long as we can see each other, be together, find out where this thing between us might go. That's all I want from you. It's all I'm asking."

Over the top of the open car door, Sarah stared at his impossibly handsome face.

Really, she didn't need any more convincing. He'd said he missed her, that he couldn't forget her. And she'd missed him, too. So very much.

No, she still didn't see him as the kind of guy who would sign on for forever with a single mom and her baby girl.

But the barriers between them were at least partly because of her. She was afraid to trust him. She'd had a little too much of men she couldn't count on and she was holding back, keeping him at a distance in order not to get hurt again.

But Logan was turning out to be so patient. He really did seem to want to be with her. He was kind and generous and he was crazy about Sophia.

Dear Reader,

IT'S A FACT: if you answer 4 quick questions, we'll send you **4 FREE REWARDS!**

I'm not kidding you. As a leading publisher of women's fiction, we value your opinions... and your time. That's why we are prepared to **reward** you handsomely for completing our mini-survey. In fact, we have 4 Free Rewards for you, including 2 free books and 2 free gifts.

As you may have guessed, that's why our mini-survey is called **"4 for 4".** Answer 4 questions and get 4 Free Rewards. It's that simple!

Thank you for participating in our survey,

Pam Powers

To get your 4 FREE REWARDS:
Complete the survey below and return the insert today to receive 2 FREE BOOKS and 2 FREE GIFTS guaranteed!

"4 for 4" MINI-SURVEY

1 Is reading one of your favorite hobbies?
YES ☐ NO ☐

2 Do you prefer to read instead of watch TV?
YES ☐ NO ☐

3 Do you read newspapers and magazines?
YES ☐ NO ☐

4 Do you enjoy trying new book series with FREE BOOKS?
YES ☐ NO ☐

YES! I have completed the above Mini-Survey. Please send me my 4 FREE REWARDS (worth over $20 retail). I understand that I am under no obligation to buy anything, as explained on the back of this card.

235/335 HDL GNU7

FIRST NAME | LAST NAME

ADDRESS

APT.# | CITY

STATE/PROV. | ZIP/POSTAL CODE

READER SERVICE—Here's how it works:

Why not just go with it, for however long it lasted? So what if it didn't go on forever? Why shouldn't she just enjoy every minute she could have with him?

Sarah stepped back. His face fell in disappointment.

But then she pushed the door shut—not all the way. She left it open enough that she would hear if Sophia started fussing.

About then, Logan must have seen her decision in her eyes. "Sarah." He said her name low, with relief. And something bordering on joy.

She moved in close. He opened his arms. And she stepped right into them, laying her hands on his broad chest, feeling his heat and the beating of his strong heart under her palms. "I'm just…scared, you know?"

His eyes turned tender, soft as the summer sky. "I know. And that's okay. Just give me a chance, anyway. Give *us* a chance."

There was a giant lump in her throat. She swallowed it down. "Okay."

One corner of that fine mouth of his hitched up. "Okay…what?"

"Okay, let's give this thing between us a fighting chance."

"You mean it?"

"Yeah. Let's do this. Let's try."

"Sarah…"

For the longest, sweetest moment, they just stared at each other.

And then, at last, he gathered her close and he kissed her, a deep, dizzying, beautiful kiss. She let her hands glide up to encircle his neck and kissed him right back.

Someone was clapping behind her. Someone else

whistled. Logan lifted his head and said, "Get lost, you kids."

She glanced over her shoulder in time to see a couple of local boys run off down the street in the same direction the two older ladies had gone.

"All right," he said, putting a finger under her chin and guiding her face back around so she met those fine blue eyes of his. "Where were we?"

She grinned up at him. "Tonight?" she asked.

"Where and when?"

"My house. Six o'clock."

Chapter Seven

Sarah turned from Sophia's crib.

Logan was waiting in the open doorway.

He held out his hand. She went to him and he wrapped his arms loosely around her. "Well?" he whispered.

She put two fingers against his lips and mouthed, "Sound asleep."

He caught her hand. "Come on."

She turned off the light and silently shut the door behind them.

After one step, he stopped in the middle of her tiny hallway. "Wait."

She gazed up at him, confused. "What?"

"This." Pulling her close, he lowered his mouth to hers.

She giggled a little against his warm lips. And then she sighed in dizzy pleasure as he kissed her more deeply. It felt so fine, so absolutely right, to be held in those lean, strong arms of his, to have his lips moving on hers, his tongue exploring her mouth in the most delicious way.

When he lifted his head and gazed down at her, she saw his desire in his eyes. Her bedroom was two steps away. And all at once, what would happen between them tonight was breathtakingly, scarily real. Her heart rate kicked up a notch. She could feel her pulse beating in her neck. He regarded her without wavering, his eyes full of promises, his mouth a little swollen from that beautiful, lingering kiss they'd just shared.

"I haven't, um, been with anyone," she said, every nerve in her body hyperactive, quivering. "Not since that conference in Denver when I got pregnant with Sophia."

He put his hands on her shoulders, so gently, in reassurance. "You're not sure."

"I didn't say that."

He stroked his palms down her arms in a soothing caress. "How about we make popcorn, stream a movie or something?"

She stared up at him, studying him, memorizing him—the fine lines around his eyes, his square jaw, that mouth she couldn't wait to kiss again. His cheeks were smooth tonight, free of the usual sexy layer of scruff. It pleased her to picture him shaving, a towel wrapped around his lean waist, getting ready for his evening with her.

And her nerves? They were easing, settling. "Not a chance." She offered a hand and he took it, weaving his fingers together with hers. "This way," she said.

In her bedroom, she turned the lamp on low. The

baby monitor was already waiting in there, the screen dark until sound or movement activated it.

"So will it be that gray-blue or the bluish-green color?" He was staring at the paint colors she'd stroked on the white wall.

She stepped in close to him and got to work unbuttoning his dove-gray shirt. "I have to tell you, at this moment, paint colors don't interest me in the least."

Now he was looking directly at her again and it felt like just maybe he could see into her heart, see her tender, never-quite-realized hopes, her slightly tarnished dreams. "Gotcha." And he kissed her, another slow, deep one.

She sighed and melted into him, surrendering to the moment, letting him take the lead.

He claimed control so smoothly, easing her into the glory of right now, his lips moving against hers, his big hands skating over her, stroking her, quieting every worry. Banishing every fear.

She let him undress her. He did it slowly, with care, taking time to kiss her and touch her as he peeled away each separate item of clothing. Time kind of faded away, along with the last of her nervous fears. He laid her down on her bed and she gazed up at him, wondering at the perfection of this moment, the hazy, sweet beauty of it.

He took his phone from one pocket, a short chain of condoms from another and set them all on the night table by the lamp. After that, he took off his own clothes swiftly, revealing his body, so lean and sharply cut. Such a fine-looking man. Everywhere. In every way.

"Is this really happening?" she asked him when he came down to her.

"You'd better believe it." He pulled her close, skin to skin. "At last."

And he kissed her some more, kisses that managed both to soothe and excite her. He kissed her all over, whispering naughty things, his lips skimming down the side of her throat, pausing to press a deeper kiss in the curve where her neck met her shoulder, sucking at her skin in that tender spot, bringing the blood to the surface.

But not stopping there. Oh, no.

He went lower, lingering first at her breasts, making her moan for him, making her cry out his name.

Swept up in sensation, she forgot all about the ways her body had changed with pregnancy, the new softness at her belly, the white striations where her skin had made room for the baby within her—until he kissed them, brushing his lips over them, so sweet and slow. She lifted her head when he did that, blinking down at him, not really believing that any man would linger over stretch marks.

He glanced up and met her eyes. And he winked at her.

She laughed and let her head fall back against the pillow.

He continued his journey, dropping kisses on the crests of her hipbones, nibbling across her lower abdomen, eventually lifting her left thigh onto his shoulder so that he could slide underneath it and settle between her legs.

Intimate, arousing, perfect kisses followed. The man

knew what he was doing. He invaded her most secret places.

And she let him. She welcomed him, opening her legs wider, reaching down to spear her fingers in his thick, short hair, urging him on, begging for more, losing herself to the sheer pleasure of his mouth, of the things that he did with those big, knowing hands of his.

She went over the edge, losing herself completely, crying out his name.

And he? Well, he just went on kissing her, touching her, stroking her, luring her right to the edge again...

And on over for the second time.

By then, she was vanquished in the best way possible, limp and so satisfied. She simply lay there, sighing, as he eased out from between her open thighs, rose to his knees above her and reached for a condom.

"Hey." His voice was low, a little raspy, teasing and coaxing.

"Hmm?" She managed a lazy smile.

"You okay?"

"Oh, Logan. Yes, I am. No, wait. On second thought, 'okay' doesn't even come close. I'm much better than okay. I'm excellent. Satisfied. Perfectly content. And ready for more." She lifted a lazy arm and reached out to him.

He took her fingers, bent closer and pressed those wonderful lips of his to the back of her hand. "That's what I wanted to hear." He let go of her to suit up, the beautiful muscles of his arms and chest flexing and bunching as he did so.

Then he braced his hands on the mattress on either

side of her and lowered himself down to her, taking care not to put all his weight on her at once.

But she wanted that—all of him, pressing her down.

"Come here. Come closer." She took those broad, hard shoulders and pulled him down.

He gave in to her urging, settling on her carefully, taking her mouth again, kissing her slowly, tasting her own arousal, reminding her sharply of how much she wanted him, of his skill as a lover, which was absolutely stunning in the best sort of way.

She felt him, large and hard and ready. And she wanted him. All of him, with nothing held back.

Did she believe that her dreams would come true with him?

No.

Something had broken in her, after Tuck and then the disappointment of Mercer. It wasn't the men, really—how could it be? She hadn't understood Tuck at all. And Mercer, well, she hardly knew the guy.

No. It wasn't the men. It was about her, about her absolute belief in her plan for her future. She'd been so very sure she had it all figured out, that she wouldn't be like her parents, settling for a colorless, nothing life in her hometown. She would have everything—great success, true love and beautiful children in the big, exciting city, because she knew what she wanted and how to get it.

But what *had* she known, really?

Nothing, that's what. She'd gone forth in arrogance, ready to conquer the world. And nothing had worked out the way she'd intended.

So no. She wasn't thinking she would get forever with Logan. She wasn't counting on anything.

For her, it was all about right now, here in her bed, with this beautiful man. Having him in her arms, wanting her, holding her.

This moment was what mattered. It was way more than enough.

He was right there, pressing, hot and insistent, where she wanted him so very much. She eased her thighs wider, wrapped her legs around him.

He groaned her name as he filled her.

"Yes," she answered. "Oh, Logan, yes..."

And then they were moving, rocking together and her mind was a white-hot blank of pure pleasure. He made it last for the longest, sweetest time. She clung to him, feeling her body rise again. When she hit the crest, she cried out at the sheer joy of it.

He followed soon after, holding her so tight.

For a while, they just lay there, arms and legs entangled, whispering together, reveling in afterglow.

As for what would happen next, what the future might bring, none of that mattered. For now, for tonight, she belonged to Logan.

And he was hers.

Thursday was the Fourth of July.

They had breakfast together at the cottage—Sarah, Sophia and Logan. He filled more pages of her notebook with sketches of Sarah at the stove flipping pancakes and then of Sophia in her bouncy seat, laughing and waving her little arms.

In the late afternoon, Sarah dressed her baby in red,

white and blue, and the three of them joined their neighbors in Rust Creek Falls Park for a community barbecue. Sarah's parents were there and Lily was, too. They all sat together on a big blanket Sarah had brought. When it came time to eat, they shared a picnic table. Everybody wanted to hold the baby. Sophia loved the attention. She hardly fussed at all, even dropping off to sleep in her baby seat when she got tired.

Laura Crawford, Nate Crawford's mom, who was a fixture behind the counter at Crawford's General Store, stopped by to chat with Sarah's mom and dad. Sophia was awake again by then and Mrs. Crawford asked to hold her.

"She's such a good baby," the older woman said as Sophia grabbed her finger and tried to use it as a teething toy. Laura Crawford glanced at Logan. "And she has your eyes."

For a second, Sarah's skin felt too hot and her pulse started racing. She felt thoroughly dissed. Surely everyone in town knew that she was a single mom and that Logan Crawford—a relative of Laura's, after all—was not her baby daddy.

But Laura wasn't a mean person. Most likely, she just meant it in a teasing way, because Logan and Sophia both had blue eyes and Sarah and Logan were making no secret of their current coupled-up status.

And what did it matter what Laura Crawford actually thought? Sarah intended to enjoy every minute of her time with Logan. A random remark by Nate Crawford's mom wasn't going to make her feel bad about herself or her choices.

Clearly, Logan wasn't bothered in the least. He

grinned at Laura. "You noticed," he said, at which point Sophia decided she wanted him to hold her.

"Ah, da!" the baby crowed, reaching out her arms to Logan, falling toward him.

Logan jumped up to catch her as Mrs. Crawford reluctantly let her go. Once he had Sophia safely in his arms, she patted his cheek and babbled out more happy nonsense.

A little later, Flo and Mack said they were going on home. Flo volunteered to take Sophia. "Stay for the dancing," she told Sarah. "You can pick the baby up on your way home. Or if it gets too late, she can just stay with us. Come get her first thing in the morning."

"Thanks, Mom." Really, it was nice. To have her mom and dad close by—especially her mom and dad the way they were now, happy and kind of easygoing, fun to be around. Sarah was even starting to get used to her mother's new frankness about sex and relationships. If Flo and Mack would just quit exploring their new sexual freedom at the office, Sarah would have zero complaints when it came to her parents.

She handed over all the baby paraphernalia and promised to come pick Sophia up by ten thirty that night.

"Or in the morning," her mom offered again. "That's fine, too."

As the band started tuning up, Sarah, Logan and Lily sat and chatted. Logan's brothers Xander and Wilder joined them. They all joked about Max and his scheme to get his boys married off.

Xander said to Logan, "At least Dad seems to be making progress with you."

Sarah sighed. Xander so didn't get it. Max wanted Logan married, yeah—just not to her. She looked away and reminded herself that she had no business feeling hurt.

So what if Max didn't consider her a good match for Logan? It wasn't like she was picking out china patterns and dreaming of monogramming her towels with a capital *C*. She and Logan were going to take it day by day and she was perfectly happy about that.

"Hey." Logan leaned in close.

She turned to him. "Hmm?"

And he kissed her, right there under the darkening sky in front of everyone on the Fourth of July in Rust Creek Falls Park. It was a quick kiss, but tender. And so very sweet.

Whatever happened, however it ended, she would remember this moment, sitting on the red, white and blue quilt her grandmother had made years and years ago, Logan's warm lips brushing hers in affection and reassurance.

"Hey, guys. What's up?" Genevieve Lawrence, in a yellow dress and cowboy boots, dropped down on the blanket next to Xander. She gave Logan's brother a radiant smile and then turned to Logan. "So, I see you took my advice."

Sarah didn't know Genevieve well, but she knew that the pretty, outgoing blonde was a true craftswoman, a farrier who trimmed and shod horses' hooves for a living. "What advice?"

Logan leaned close again. "Date number two," he whispered.

"Ah." She asked again, "What advice?"

Genevieve pretended to smooth her flared skirt. "It's all good, I promise." She wiggled her eyebrows at Sarah. "Make him tell you when you're alone."

Right then, the band launched into Lady Antebellum's "American Honey."

Genevieve turned to Xander. "How 'bout a dance?"

Xander jumped up, offered his hand and led the energetic blonde to the portable dance floor set up under the trees just as the party lights strung from branch to branch came on over their heads.

A moment later, another girl wandered over. Sarah vaguely recognized her, but couldn't recall her name.

Not that it mattered. The girl asked Wilder to dance and off they went.

Lily watched them go, a wistful look on her face.

Sarah slid a glance at Logan. Their eyes met and it was as though he'd read her mind.

"Want to dance, Lily?"

Lily smoothed her pulled-back hair. "You should dance with Sarah."

He only gazed at Lily steadily and asked again, "Dance with me?"

Sarah said, "Looks like he's not takin' no for an answer, Lil."

"Oh, you two." Lily waved her hand in front of her face.

But when Logan got up and held down his hand, she took it.

As they danced, Logan asked Sarah's friend about her job at Maverick Manor.

Lily said she loved to cook and she really wished she

could get more hours. "But as of now, I'm part-time. Hey. At least it's something."

Cole and Viv Dalton danced by. Viv smiled at Logan.

He nodded in response and glanced down at Sarah's friend again. "So, have you joined Viv Dalton's dating service yet?"

Lily scoffed. "Yeah. Like that's gonna happen."

"Why not? I can personally vouch for each of my brothers. They can be troublesome and maybe a little rough around the edges, but they're all good at heart, not to mention good-looking. One of them could be the guy for you."

"Seems to me they've got plenty of women to choose from already."

"Give it a chance, Lily. What have you got to lose? If nothing else, you might have a good time."

She frowned up at him, but her eyes gleamed with wry humor. "Logan Crawford, you are much too persuasive."

"Just think about it."

She shrugged. "Sure. I'll do that."

Did he believe her? Not really. And that created the strangest urge in him to keep pushing her—because he liked her and she mattered to Sarah and he really did think it would be good for her, to get out there and mix it up a little.

On the other hand, it was none of his damn business whether Lily Hunt went out with one of his brothers or not. He'd said more than enough about the wedding planner's dating pool.

When the dance ended, he and Lily rejoined Sarah on the blanket. Hunter and Wren wandered over and sat down with them. Max stopped by. Logan prepared to get tough on his dad if he gave Sarah any grief. But Max was on his best behavior, greeting both Sarah and Lily in an easy, friendly way, going on about how great it was to spend Independence Day with the good citizens of his new hometown.

The band started playing another slow one. Logan leaned close to Sarah and breathed in her delicate scent. "Let's dance."

"Yes." Her eyes shone so bright and he was the happiest man in Montana, just to be spending his Fourth of July at her side.

She gave him her hand. They rose together.

Max got up, too. "I think I'll go check in with Viv and Cole. Great to meet you, Lily." He aimed a too-wide smile at Logan. "We need you out at the Ambling A good and early tomorrow."

"I'll be there."

"Fences to mend, cattle to tend," Max added in a jovial tone that set Logan's teeth on edge.

He always did his share of the work and Max knew it, too. Ignoring the temptation to mutter something sarcastic, Logan led Sarah to the dance floor, where he wrapped his arms around her and didn't let go through that song and the next and the next after that.

A little later, they rolled up her grandmother's quilt and wandered over to Rust Creek, which meandered through the center of town. The local merchants association had arranged for a fireworks display right there at creekside. Everyone sat around on the grass and watched the bright explosions light up the night sky.

It was after eleven when the fireworks show ended.

Logan and Sarah strolled by her parents' house on the way to Sarah's place, just on the off-chance that her mom and dad might still be up. All the lights were off.

Sarah said it was fine. She would pick up Sophia in the morning. Holding hands, they strolled on to her cottage, where she hesitated before leading him up the front walk.

"I know you have to be up and working early," she said.

He had the quilt under one arm, but he pulled her close with the other hand. "Are you trying to get rid of me?"

She gazed up at him, her mouth so tempting, the moon reflected in her eyes. "No way."

"Good, then. I'll get up before dawn and sneak out. I promise not to wake you." He wrapped his free arm around her and claimed a quick, hard kiss.

Laughing softly, she led him up the walk.

Sarah woke at six fifteen the next morning.

Logan's side of the bed was empty. She slid her hand over there. The sheet was cool.

Longing warmed her belly and made her throat tight. Last night had been every bit as beautiful and fulfilling as the night before. He'd made love to her twice and she'd dropped off to sleep with a smile on her face.

Already, she was getting so attached to him. She should probably claim a little space between them, let a few days go by at least, before seeing him again.

But then she got up and went into the kitchen and found a drawing of a weathered fence, a barn in the background and a sign hooked to the fence that read, *See you tonight. 6 o'clock. I'll bring takeout.*

And her plans to get some distance? Gone like morning mist at sunrise.

Grinning to herself, she grabbed her phone and texted him.

There had better not be candles or fine china involved in your takeout plans this time. She paused without sending and frowned at the text box before adding, You know what? Forget takeout. I'll fix us something. She hit Send, figuring it would be a while before he had a chance to check his phone.

Not so.

He came right back with, I'll stop at Daisy's and get dessert.

That evening, he arrived right on time carrying a bakery box full of red velvet cupcakes with cream cheese frosting. Then he kept Sophia busy while Sarah got the dinner on. When they sat down to eat, he held Sophia in his lap. With one hand, he helped her keep hold of her bottle. With the other, he ate his chicken and oven-roasted potatoes.

Once Sophia was in bed, he led Sarah straight to her bedroom. He removed her clothes and his, too, in record time and then did a series of truly wonderful things to her body.

Later, after she'd turned off the lamp, as she drifted toward sleep, feeling so safe and satisfied and peaceful, her head on his chest and those hard arms around her, he said, "You need to choose your paint colors. I talked to the guy at the paint store in Kalispell. I can order the paint and he'll send it over with a couple of professional painters. They'll get the job done the way you want it."

She didn't know whether she felt bulldozed or taken

care of. "Logan, I don't want to spend my money on professional painters."

He smoothed a hand down her hair and pressed a kiss on the top of her head. "That's okay. I'm going to pay for the paint *and* the guys to do the painting."

She wiggled out of his grip, sat up and turned on the lamp. "No, you're not."

"Sarah," he chided gently. "Yes, it's true that now I spend my working days moving cattle and repairing farm equipment, but that's by choice."

"Back to the land and all that, huh?"

"Essentially, yeah. What I'm saying is I've got money to burn."

"Good for you, Mr. Moneybags. I don't."

"Exactly. So let me do this for you. Don't make a big issue of it."

"But it *is* an issue, Logan."

"It doesn't have to be."

She sat there and glared at him, more annoyed by the second. "How can you possibly be so wonderful and so pigheaded simultaneously?"

He pretended to give that some thought. "I'm getting the feeling the question is rhetorical."

"Let me make this achingly clear—no. You are not paying for the paint *or* the painters."

He studied her, his blue eyes narrowed. "You need it done. I want to do it for you. This shouldn't be a problem."

"Listen carefully. Thank you for the offer, but I will do this my way."

He didn't answer immediately, which gave her hope that he had finally let it go. And then he reached out, slid his big, rough hand up under her hair and hooked it around the back of her neck. A gentle tug and she was pressed up against him.

She glanced up to meet his eyes. And his mouth came down on hers. He kissed her slowly. By the time he lifted his head again she was feeling all fluttery inside.

"So what's the compromise?" he asked. "How about a painting party?"

She reached over and turned off the light. They settled back down, her head on his chest. She traced a heart on his shoulder. "Hmm. A painting party..."

"You like that?" He sounded way too pleased with himself. "We could at least get a room or two painted, depending on how many people we could get and how long we all worked."

"When would this painting party occur?"

"A week from tomorrow—or sooner, depending on when everyone can come? We could make a list of victims—I mean, volunteers. We'll paint and then feed everybody. I'm thinking pizza and Wings To Go, soft drinks, beer and wine."

"I'll buy my own paint and supplies."

"Hey, you're the boss."

"Yes, I am and you shouldn't forget it."

"I'll bring the food and drinks," he said. She would have argued, but he added, "Shh. Let me do that, at least."

"All right." She lifted up and kissed him. "Thank you."

The next day was Saturday. Well before dawn, she woke to an empty bed. But then a floorboard creaked and she saw him through the shadows. He was pulling on his jeans.

She sat up, flicked on the lamp and yawned. "Don't you take Saturday off?"

One shoulder lifted in a half shrug. "There's always work that needs doing around the Ambling A."

"You can't possibly be getting enough sleep."

He zipped his fly. A little thrill shivered through her when he looked up and met her eyes. Whatever this was between them, however long it lasted, it sure did feel good. "I set my own hours. Today, I'll only work until around three," he said, "and then I'll get a nap. I'm fine, believe me. I'll be back at six tonight."

She just sat there with the covers pulled up over her bare breasts, thinking he was the best-looking guy she'd ever seen. "I'll do something with the leftover chicken. I mean it, Logan. Don't bring anything. There are still some cupcakes left for dessert."

He'd picked up his shirt, but then he dropped it again and stalked to the bed. Spearing his fingers in her scrambled hair, he hauled her close and kissed her, a deep, slow kiss, morning breath be damned.

When he let her go, she laughed. She couldn't help it—really, she laughed a lot when he was around. "Did you hear what I said?"

"Every word."

Maybe. But that didn't mean he would do as she asked. "You are impossible."

"And you mean that in the *best* possible way, am I right?"

"Yeah, right." She admired the gorgeous musculature

of his back as he returned to the chair and scooped up his shirt again. Then she frowned. "Hold on a minute."

He turned as he was slipping his arms in the sleeves and she was presented with that amazing sculpted chest and corrugated belly. "Yeah?"

"I just remembered. I usually try not to schedule appointments on the weekends, but I have a quarterly report to go over with a shoe store owner in Kalispell. We were supposed to meet yesterday, but he asked if I could move our meeting to today. It could go as late as six or six thirty."

"No problem. I'll wait."

"What? Like on the front porch?" That didn't seem right.

He dropped to the chair and pulled on a sock. "Sarah, it's not a big deal." He put on the other sock and reached for a boot.

"No. Really. There's an extra house key in that little green bowl on the entry table. Take it. Let yourself in if I'm not here when you arrive."

"That works." He pulled on the other boot and stood to button his shirt and tuck it in. Then he came to her again, tipped up her chin and gave her another sweet kiss. "Lie down. Go back to sleep." He waited for her to stretch out under the covers and then tucked them in around her.

"Drive carefully," she whispered.

"I will." He turned off the light.

She listened to his quiet footfalls as he left the room. A minute later, she heard the soft click of the lock as he went out the front door and then, very faintly, his crew cab starting up and driving away.

For a while, she lay awake, staring into the shadows, thinking how she didn't want to start depending on him, couldn't afford to get overly involved with him. She wasn't ready to go risking her heart again.

And yet, she'd gone and given him a key to her house.

Chapter Eight

Logan worked alone that day setting posts to fence a pasture several miles from the ranch house. It was good, being out on his own. He got a lot done when there was no one else around to distract him with idle talk and suggestions about how this or that task should be done.

Being on his own also gave him time to think—about Sarah, about this thing they had going on between them.

When it came to Sarah, he didn't really know what exactly was happening to him.

There was just something about her. From the first moment he'd set eyes on her that day at the old train depot, he'd only wanted to get closer to her, get to know her better.

It wasn't like him. He adored women, but he'd always

been careful not to get attached to any of them, not to let them worm their way into his heart.

There had been some hard lessons in his childhood and those lessons had stuck.

Logan was seven years old when his mom abandoned her family to run off with her lover. Max had said really cruel things about her then, called her rotten names. He'd told Logan and his brothers to get used to her being gone because she'd deserted them without a backward glance and she was never coming home. He'd said that a man couldn't trust any woman, and it was better for all his boys that they were learning that lesson early.

At the time, Logan refused to believe that he would never see his mom again. How could he believe it? Until she vanished from their lives without a hint of warning, Sheila had been a good mom, gentle and understanding, always there when he or his brothers needed her. For years, into his middle teens, he refused to lose faith in her basic goodness, in the devotion he just knew she felt to him and to his brothers. No matter what his dad said, he was waiting for her to return.

But she never did. She never so much as reached out. Not a letter or a phone call. Nothing. Radio silence. Year after year after year.

On his fifteenth birthday, when once again she didn't call or even send a card, he finally got it. He accepted the hard truth. Max was right. Sheila was gone for good and he needed to stop waiting for her to change her mind and return to her family.

That day—the day he turned fifteen—he finally accepted the lesson Max had tried so hard to teach him. A guy needed to protect himself, because if you let her, a woman would rip your heart out and leave you with nothing, dead and empty inside.

By then, it didn't matter that logically he knew it was beyond wrong to blame all women because his mother had deserted her family. Logic didn't even figure into it. The lesson of self-protection had hardwired itself into his brain, wrapped itself like barbwire around his heart.

Of course, he knew that there had to be lots of women in the world who kept their promises and took care of their own above all. He just didn't see any reason to go looking for one of them. He liked life on his own.

And in the years that followed, Logan never allowed himself to get too close to anyone. He was more of an overnight meaningful relationship kind of guy, a guy who treated any woman he was with like a queen for as long as it lasted—which was never very long. He always made it clear to any woman who caught his eye that he wasn't a man she should pin her hopes on.

But with Sarah…

It was different with her from the first moment he saw her that day at the train depot. To him, there had seemed to be a glow around her. As though she had a light inside her, a beacon that drew him inexorably closer.

Part of her attraction at first was her very wariness with him. No need to protect himself when she was doing such a bang-up job of pushing him away.

She made it so clear that she didn't want anything from him, wouldn't accept anything from him and would never let him get too close to her. That deep reserve in her just made him want her more.

Because honestly, what man wouldn't want Sarah—

with that slow-blooming smile of hers, those golden-brown eyes, that long, thick hair streaked with bronze, her softly rounded curves and her scent of flowers and elusive spice?

He'd been miserable when she ended it before it ever really got started. And then, when she admitted she wanted to try again, he'd been over the damn moon.

And now, this morning, she'd given him a key.

A key, damn it. That should have been enough to have him backing out the door with his hands up, shaking his head, apologizing for giving her the wrong idea. That should have had him drawing the line, saying no, absolutely not. He wasn't a man who ever took a woman's key.

Which reminded him. He'd never had "the talk" with her, never said that he really liked her but she needed to know he wasn't looking for anything serious.

He'd never had the talk and he wasn't going to have the talk. If he did that, he knew exactly what she would say—goodbye. The last thing Sarah needed was reminding that what they had wasn't permanent. She already knew that.

Better than he did.

No, with Sarah, goodbye didn't work for him. He wasn't anywhere near ready to walk away from her.

Did he expect it to last with her?

He kept telling himself he didn't.

But all that day as he set posts for new fences, he couldn't stop thinking about her, about that smile she had that lit up her whole face, about the way she cared for Sophia, always putting the baby first, taking her everywhere, managing to run a business with Sophia in tow. Maybe that was what made Sophia such a happy, trusting little thing. Maybe even a baby knew when she could count on her mother absolutely.

And what about the way Sarah didn't want him to give her things or do things for her?

Well, that only made him want to do more, to give her more. He was having a great time just coming up with new ways to make her life a little easier, to bring a smile to that pretty face of hers, to make her laugh, make her sigh. He had this weird dedication to Sarah *and* to Sophia, to their well-being, their happiness.

Was he in too deep?

Definitely.

Would she mess him over?

God, he hoped not.

Because somehow, with Sarah, he seemed to have misplaced his hard-earned instinct for self-preservation.

Sarah didn't get home that night until ten minutes of seven. Logan's pickup was already there, parked at the curb. She turned into her narrow driveway and got out to open the door of the cottage's detached garage. But before she could do that, Logan emerged from the house.

"I'll get it," he called and jogged across her small plot of lawn to open the door for her.

She got back in behind the wheel and parked in the dim little space. Logan went around and got Sophia in her carrier out of the back seat as Sarah grabbed the diaper bag and tote and got out, too. He shut the garage door and they walked across the lawn and up the front steps together.

At the front door, he reached out and put his hand on her arm. "Before we go in…"

Warmth filled her, just from that simple touch. She slanted him a sideways look as Sophia let out a joyful crow of baby laughter, followed by a gleeful, "Ah, da, na!"

He glanced down at her and grinned. "I'm happy to see you, too, Soph. It's been hours."

The man was a menace—to her heart and her emotional equilibrium. Really, she needed to talk to him, tell him to be a little less wonderful, please. "Before we go in, what?" she asked. His blue gaze lifted to meet hers. Now he looked…guilty, maybe? Or at least marginally apprehensive. "What did you do, Logan?"

He made a throat-clearing sound and took his free hand from her arm to rub the back of his neck. "Well, it's like this…"

She tried really hard not to grin. Because she *shouldn't* be grinning. He'd done something he knew he probably shouldn't do, something that she would have vetoed if only he'd asked her first.

How did she know that? She had no idea. Just, sometimes, she could read him simply by looking at his face.

She forced a stern expression. "I'd better not find my house painted when I go inside."

Another happy giggle from Sophia. And from Logan, "Whoa." Now he looked hurt. "I wouldn't do that. We already agreed about that."

"Okay…" She spoke the word on a rising inflection and waited for him to explain himself.

"Well, see, it was like this. As I'm on my way back to town this afternoon, I see this kid by the side of the road, a little towheaded kid in busted out jeans and a straw hat. He's sitting in a folding chair with this big cardboard box beside him and a sign that says, Kittens Free to Good Home."

She knew what he'd done then. "Logan, tell me you didn't."

He put up his free hand and patted the air with it. "Look, if you don't like her, I'll take her to the ranch, okay?"

"It's a female kitten is what you're saying and it is in my house right now."

"See, Wren might want her. Or I'll keep her for myself if I have to."

"All these options you have for where you might have taken her. And yet, you brought her here."

"Yeah. But first, I stopped at the vet. I got lucky and they were still open. I bought everything she'll need. Food and bowls, litter, a litter box, a scooper thing, a scratching post, a few toys and a bed. The kid who gave her to me said she's ten weeks old and hasn't had any shots. So I had the vet give them to her—along with a checkup. She's a healthy little girl, no sign of fleas. And she'll need her next shots in three to four weeks."

"Thought of everything, did you?"

"Sarah." He'd adopted his most reasonable, placating tone. "Don't be mad, okay? I meant what I said. I don't expect you to keep her."

For some reason, she wanted to burst out laughing. He looked so worried and she was having way too much fun giving him a hard time about this.

And as for the kitten, the last thing she needed was another baby to care for. However...

"When I was a kid, I always wanted a cat," she heard herself saying.

His eyes went soft as the midsummer sky. "You did?"

"My parents didn't allow pets. As I mentioned that first day in the office at the Ambling A, my parents were different back then. But I'm not saying I'll keep her."

He put his hand to his heart. "What did I tell you? If you don't want her, I'll take her with me tomorrow when I go."

So then, he was staying overnight again? She had no urge to argue about that. In fact, she was glad. Probably gladder than she should let herself be. "Does this kitten have a name?"

"Not yet. I figured you would want to name her yourself—I mean, if you decide to keep her."

"How thoughtful of you."

Now he grinned. "Knock it off with the sarcasm. You just admitted you like cats. And I'm telling you, you're not going to be able to resist this one." And with that, he pushed open the door and signaled her in ahead of him.

She saw the tiny kitten immediately. All white, with a perfect pink nose and ears, and the prettiest, blue-opal eyes, she sat beneath the dining area table. "Oh, my God," Sarah heard herself whisper. "She's adorable."

Those gorgeous, wide eyes regarded her from that perfect little face.

Setting her laptop on the coffee table and letting the diaper bag slide to the carpet, Sarah dropped to a crouch. "Hey there." She held out her hand. "Come here, you little angel. Come on…"

The kitten dipped her head to the side, considering.

"Reow?" she said as though asking a question, but she didn't budge.

"Such a pretty girl." She coaxed, "Come on, come here..."

That did it. The kitten stood. Delicately, she stretched her front legs and widened her paws. White whiskers twitching, she yawned. And then finally, after a few extra seconds of ladylike hesitation, she strutted out from under the table. White tail high, she paraded across the dining room and straight for Sarah, stopping when she reached her to delicately sniff her outstretched fingers.

Sarah waited until the kitten dropped to her butt again before daring to reach out. The kitten was already purring. Sarah pulled her close. Cradling the little snowball against her heart, she stood.

From behind her, Logan chuckled. "So then, what's her name?"

"Opal," she said without turning, bending her head to nuzzle the kitten's wonderfully soft fur. "Opal, for those eyes."

"Thank you for Opal," Sarah said. It was a little past eleven that night. They were tucked up in bed together and had been for a couple of beautiful hours. Earlier, after sharing dinner, they'd made the calls to set up the painting party for next week. Sophia had been asleep since eight or so. With any luck, she wouldn't wake up until daylight.

As for the kitten in question, Opal was sleeping in her new bed in the laundry room with the litter box close by. Sarah had wanted to bring her to bed with them, but the vet had advised Logan that she should sleep in her own bed with easy access to her litter box until she got a little older.

Logan chuckled. The sound was a lovely rumble beneath Sarah's left ear because she was using his warm, hard chest for a pillow. "I knew you would want her." He eased his fingers into her hair and idly combed it outward over her shoulders and down her back. "And I've been thinking…"

She stacked her hands on his chest and rested her chin on them. "Uh-oh. What now?"

"You need an electric garage-door opener."

She lifted up enough to plant a kiss on his square, beard-scruffy jaw. "No, I do not."

"Yeah, you really do. And when winter comes, you know you'll thank me. You don't need to be staggering around on your icy driveway trying to get the garage door up."

"There will be staggering whether I have an electric opener or not. I still have to make it from the garage to the house."

"Right." He was frowning. "And you'll be carrying Sophia and a laptop in that giant bag of yours—and that diaper bag, too. It's too dangerous."

"Logan, let it be."

"A side door to the garage and an enclosed breezeway leading around to the back door would fix the problem. No matter how bad the weather gets, you and Sophia would be safe and protected."

"That's a major project, Logan."

"Just let me deal with it. It's not that big a thing."

It *was* a big thing. Really, he was relentless—and in the most wonderful way. "Stop. I mean it. Let it go."

He guided a lock of hair back over her shoulder with a slow, gentle touch. "Think about it."

She needed to change the subject, fast. And she knew exactly how to do it. They'd already made love twice.

Time to go for number three.

Lifting up again, she pressed her lips to his. He let out a low growl of pleasure as he opened for her. She eased her tongue in, sliding it slowly against his.

His arms banded around her, so hot and hard. "You're trying to distract me," he grumbled.

She caught his lower lip between her teeth and worried it a little. "Yes, I am. Is it working?"

"I still want you to have that garage-door opener." His voice was rough now, his breathing just a tad ragged.

She slid her hand down between them and encircled his hard length. He groaned aloud and she asked in a teasing purr, "Do I have your attention, Logan?"

He released a hard breath. "Sarah…" A harsh word escaped him.

"No. Garage. Door. Opener," she instructed, low and firmly, making each word a sentence. "Got that?"

"I do, yeah." Another groan escaped him. "I definitely do."

"Good, then." She captured his mouth as she stroked him, holding on tight, increasing the pressure, working her hand up and down on him—until he turned the tables, wrapping an arm around her and deftly flipping her over so that she was beneath him. He levered up and reached for a condom.

A moment later, she held him within her, all the way.

She stared up into his blue, blue eyes, feeling cherished. Happy. And so very aroused.

When he started to move, she forgot everything but the pleasure of the moment.

Who knew what would happen as the days went by? She didn't know and she really didn't care.

It didn't work to count on a man, not for her. She'd learned that the hard way.

So she wasn't counting on him. She was simply enjoying herself, having the best time, just being with him, being Sarah and Logan, together, for right now.

Sunday, Sarah had no appointments and Logan decided to take a day off.

He stayed for breakfast. Then he herded her and Sophia to his crew cab and drove them to Kalispell, where the paint store he'd chosen opened at ten.

They bought paint and painting supplies. He convinced her to go ahead and buy the paint for all the rooms, even though they would only be tackling Sophia's room and the kitchen during the painting party next week. The bill for all that was pretty steep, but she really did want to get it done.

Of course, he had to offer, "Change your mind. Let me take care of it." She just shook her head and handed the paint store guy her credit card.

Logan wanted to take them out to lunch, but Sophia was a little fussy and Sarah kind of wanted to get back and see how Opal was doing. They bought takeout from a Chinese place they both liked and returned to Rust Creek Falls. After lunch, while Sophia was napping, he suggested they paint one of the rooms.

She cast an anxious eye at the cans of paint and supplies taking up most of the space in her dining room. "I know nothing about painting and the more I think about it, the more I kind of have a bad feeling about this."

He reacted with an easy shrug. "Well, great. I'll call in the professionals."

"Don't even go there." She sent him her sternest frown. "We've been through that more than once and it's not happening."

"So, then, we paint."

"Ugh. You are way too upbeat about this."

He hooked an arm around her and gave her an encouraging squeeze. "Piece of cake, I promise you."

"Oh, like you're some kind of expert?"

"Well, I worked for a house painter part-time during college to earn extra cash and when I first got to Seattle, I flipped houses. To save money, I painted the interiors myself."

She gaped up at him. "It's kind of not fair how much you know about a bunch of random things."

"I'm a Renaissance man, no doubt about it." He kissed the tip of her nose. "Look. You said you don't need to do the ceilings or the trim, right?"

"Yeah. The white ceilings are fine. And the cream-colored trim still looks fresh. I think my mom said they had the place painted a couple of years back."

"So, it's going to be easy." He gave her a thoroughly self-confident smirk.

"You say that with such conviction."

"Because it's true. The trim takes the longest and we're not doing the trim."

"I'm kind of worried we don't have enough tape."

"No problem. We won't need to tape."

"That's crazy. We'll get paint on the trim."

"No, we won't. You can do the rolling and I'll use a brush to cut in—meaning frame everything out, do all the parts that are too tight for a roller..."

"But—"

"Shh. No buts. I've done a lot of cutting-in and I won't get paint on your trim."

He seemed so confident, she agreed to do it his way.

Lily showed up just after they'd finished pushing the living and dining room furniture away from the walls and covering everything with plastic drop cloths.

"I'm going to help," Lily declared. "I'll just run home and change." In no time, she was back wearing worn jeans and a frayed T-shirt. Logan gave her a quick lesson in how to use a roller and she went to work.

Then Sarah's mom showed up with a plastic container full of sugar cookies. They took a cookie break. Sophia woke up and started fussing, so Flo went and got her, fed her and changed her—and then stuck around to watch her and to keep Opal out of the paint trays.

At some point, Flo called a couple of her friends and Sarah's dad, too. They all came over to pitch in. As it turned out, Sarah's dad and one of Flo's friends both had painting experience. They joined Logan to do the detail work. The rest of them used the rollers.

By seven that night, they'd finished the living room, the dining room, Sarah's room, the hallway and the bath—everything but the two rooms slated for next Saturday's painting party. They even cleaned up, washing rollers and brushes, removing drop cloths and putting all the furniture back where it belonged.

Sarah's mom invited everyone to her house for slow-cooker pot roast. As a group, they walked over to Flo and Mack's house, with Flo pushing Sophia in her stroller.

On arrival, Flo served them all pot roast, with home-made ice cream for dessert. Sarah found it weirdly disorienting, eating dinner in her mother's dining room, everybody chattering and laughing, having a great time. It was so unlike the way things used to be when she was growing up.

That night, after Sophia was in bed, Sarah and Logan streamed a Western on her laptop. Opal joined them on the sofa, snuggling in close to Sarah. The room, now a soothing gray-green, looked amazing. Sarah spent more time staring around her in wonderment than she did watching the movie.

"I think you like the new paint," Logan said as the credits started rolling. She leaned forward to shut down the laptop on the coffee table in front of them. When she sat back, Logan wrapped his arm around her.

"I loved everything about today," she said with a sigh. Opal was curled up next to her in a fluffy white ball, sound asleep. Sarah scratched her head gently, simply to hear her purr. "It was so nice how everybody just showed up—and then stayed to help get the job done. It was really so sweet of them."

"That's the deal around here, right? Everyone pitching in, helping out."

"Yeah. I love that about Rust Creek Falls—but it was strange at my parents' today."

His arm around her tightened as he pulled her a little closer. "Why strange?"

"Well, it's just that when I was growing up, we hardly ever had people over. And the house was always deadly quiet. I felt so lonely. But now, today, everyone was talking over each other, laughing, having a great old time. My mom and dad looked so happy. Sometimes now, when I'm around them, I feel like I've dropped into an alternate universe. They aren't the Flo and Mack I used to know."

"But it's a good thing, isn't it, the way they've changed?"

She took his hand and laced their fingers together. "Yeah. It's definitely a good thing. I could really get used to this, to the way they are now. I feel…kind of close to them. And I love how they have my back now. I believe I can count on them now. Plus, I'm starting to look forward to being here for them as they're growing older." She leaned her head on his shoulder. "I mean, I dreaded coming home partly because I felt that I never had any real relationship with my parents. It was depressing just being around them, trying to do simple things like have an actual conversation with them. They were so closed-off and set in their ways. But since I've been back—well, you saw how they are with each other now."

He chuckled. "Yeah, no intimacy issues between Flo and Mack."

"Not anymore, that's for sure. It took some getting used to. But now, well, that's who they are and they're happy together. And I'm starting to be really glad about that."

He tugged on a lock of her hair. "So it's all working out."

"A lot better than I expected, yeah."

"Now, all you need is a decent TV."

She groaned and elbowed him in the side. "Don't even go there."

But he just kept on. "I'm thinking at least fifty inches. Flat screens are a steal lately. I can get one for practically nothing."

The guy was incorrigible. She leaned into him and kissed his cheek. "No. That is not happening."

He held her gaze. "I'm here all the time and I like being here."

"I like having you here."

"I also like big screens." He said it longingly.

She shouldn't let herself weaken. He did way too much for her already. But he was looking at her so wistfully, like Opal when she wanted her Fancy Feast. "It's a small living room," she said and then wanted to clap her hand over her mouth the minute she added, "Fifty inches is just too big."

One of his eyebrows inched toward his hairline. She'd just opened the door to a negotiation and he knew it, too. She could tell by that gleeful gleam in his eye. "Forty-three inches, then. That's thirty-seven and a half inches wide and just over twenty-one inches high."

She tried her best stern look—not that it ever did a bit of good with him. "I see you have all the stats on the fancy TVs."

"You know I do, baby. We can put it in that corner." He pointed at the arch to the dining area, on the right side nearest the hallway to the bedrooms. "It won't overwhelm the space, I promise you."

She was weakening. Because, really, why shouldn't he buy a nice TV? He said that money was no problem for him and she believed him. And if things didn't last between them, she could just insist that he take it back, keep it for himself.

If things didn't last…

She probably shouldn't let herself think that way. They had something special together and she was so happy.

But you just never knew in life. The whole point with her and Logan was to enjoy each other, take it one day at a time together.

He caught her chin and turned her face so that she met his eyes again. "Okay. What happened?"

"Nothing. Really."

"I was about to convince you we need to *compromise* and get a forty-three-inch TV and you suddenly got sad on me."

The man was way too perceptive. As a rule, she loved that about him. Except when he picked up on stuff there was no point in getting into.

She leaned in and kissed him, quick and hard. "I mean it. It's nothing—and okay."

His eyebrow rose again. "Okay, what?"

"Forty-three inches and not a fraction more."

He leaned even closer. His rough cheek touched her smooth one and his warm breath teased her ear. "Now, that's what I wanted to hear. Let's put Opal to bed."

"And then what?"

"I'm thinking that first we need a long, relaxing bath…"

They shared the bathtub and helped each other scrub off all the random dried paint spatters. Then they did other things. Sexy things.

By the time they were through in the tub, there was

water all over the bathroom floor. They used their bath towels to mop it up.

And then they went to bed—and right to sleep for the first time since he started spending his nights at her place. He wrapped himself around her, his front to her back. She smiled in contentment and closed her eyes...

And when she woke in the morning, he was already gone.

In the kitchen she found more sketches and a note.

I'll be back by three. I'll bring dinner—don't argue. Just takeout, I promise. And don't try to tell me it's too far to go for takeout. I'm going to Kalispell anyway. Hint: it's 43 inches and it has your name on it.

That night he set up the new TV. He'd even bought surround-sound speakers. She accused him of being extravagant.

"You're going to love it." He grabbed her hand, pulled her down into his lap and nuzzled her neck. "Now, how 'bout some popcorn?"

She popped up a big bowl of it and they watched a heist movie.

Later, in bed, he was playful, tender and demanding. Really, it was so good with him. Everything. All of it. The sex, definitely. But all the other stuff, too.

He was always looking for ways to please her, to help her, to make her life better somehow. And she liked just being with him, talking about nothing in particular. Or not even talking at all.

And Opal. That he'd given her Opal, well, that meant so much to her. The kitten was healthy, smart, affectionate and just too cute. It was as if he'd found that special something she hadn't even known she longed for, a childhood wish never realized and destined to remain unfulfilled.

Until now. Because of him.

He was so good with Sophia. Her daughter adored him.

That could be difficult if they broke up. Or was Sophia too young to miss him?

Yet again, she reminded herself not to think that way. No way was Logan considering breaking up with her any time soon. He was always saying how happy he was with her, how crazy he was for Sophia. And he proved the truth of his words in action every day. No, it probably wouldn't last forever, what Sarah had with him. But nothing ever did.

Life in Rust Creek Falls was turning out to be pretty good for her and her baby. And she needed to keep looking on the bright side of things.

The bright side most definitely included her relationship with Logan Crawford. She promised herself she would keep that firmly in mind, not let the hard lessons she'd learned from past disappointments ruin a really good thing.

For as long as it lasted, she would love every minute.

Chapter Nine

That Wednesday, Logan asked her to come on out to the ranch for a picnic dinner. Her last appointment ended early, so she arrived sooner than she'd said she would, at a little after five.

With Sophia asleep in her carrier on one arm and the always-present diaper bag slung on her other shoulder, she went up the front steps.

The door opened before she reached it.

"The lovely Sarah," said Max. "And her cute little baby." He stepped back and ushered her in.

"Where's Logan?" Sarah asked as Max shut the door behind her.

"He'll be down in a minute. Here, let me help you with that." He took the diaper bag off her shoulder and hung it on the coatrack, then he swept out a hand toward the arch that led to the living room. "Come on in. Have a seat."

She didn't trust him. But she couldn't run for cover every time Logan's dad glanced her way.

Head high, expression serene, Sarah went into the living room and took a seat on the leather sofa. She set the carrier on the cushion beside her.

Max took the big easy chair across from her. "I'm glad to have a moment with you, a little time to talk." He smiled that charming smile of his, but his eyes were cool. Calculating.

She sat up a little straighter. "Look, Max, I don't know what you're leading up to here, but—"

He cut her off with a wave of his hand. "It's simple, really. I just want to, er, touch base."

"Let me be blunt. You and I have nothing to talk about. But if you insist, I think it would better if we included Logan in whatever you're about to discuss with me."

"Now, Sarah, this is not a discussion. I only want to remind you that Logan is thirty-three and has never had a serious relationship. He's a bad bet. And for you, with a baby to think of, well, you have to see that it's unwise for you to get involved with him."

Okay, it was just possible that, given her own not-so-stellar experience with men and romance, she actually kind of agreed with Logan's dad—she'd even said as much to Lily that night at Maverick Manor. But her doubts about Logan were for her to deal with in her own mind and heart. She and Logan had an understanding. They wanted to be together for right now and that was working out beautifully for them. Max Crawford had no right to try to make her choices for her.

True, in the past, it had hurt her that Logan's dad seemed to view her as unsuitable for his oldest son simply because she had a baby. Up till now, she'd just wanted to escape, run away like a hurt child, when he treated her unkindly.

But this was becoming ridiculous. It was time she stood up to him.

Drawing her shoulders back, she folded her hands in her lap and said pleasantly, "So you're saying that Logan is a bad bet for me, but *not* for those other women you had Viv set him up with?"

Max blinked in surprise. Apparently, he hadn't expected a rational argument from her. "Ahem. You don't understand, Sarah."

"That's because you really aren't making any sense, Max."

"It's, um, for your own good and the good of your child. You should at least know the statistics on the situation."

He had statistics to convince her to walk away from Logan? Really? She asked politely, "What statistics?"

"Well, just that if a man of Logan's age hasn't been married or in a serious, committed relationship, his chances of ever getting married are very low—and if he does get married, it's not all that likely to be a marriage that lasts."

Did she believe him? Not one bit. "I have to tell you, Max. I think you just made up those 'statistics' to fit your weak argument. I mean, if Logan were over forty, yeah, I might agree. When a guy gets past forty and he's happily single, any woman could find herself wondering if he simply prefers the single life. That might make him a bad marriage bet. But a lot of men wait till their thirties to settle down, so in Logan's case, your argument doesn't apply—not that I'm hoping to settle down with Logan."

Max's eyes widened. "Er...you're not?"

"We enjoy each other's company and we're having a good time."

"I didn't, er, well..." Max was actually at a loss for words. It was a rare moment and Sarah let herself enjoy it.

"And also," she added, "if you really believe what you're telling me, that he's such a bad marriage bet, why set him up with some other poor girl when, according to your reasoning, he'll only break *her* heart in the end?"

Max hemmed and hawed. "Well, now, Sarah, I'm only trying to help you realize that—"

"What do you think you're doing, Dad?" Logan stood in the open arch to the entry hall. His hair was wet and his lean cheeks freshly shaved. The sight of him made Sarah's heart ache in the sweetest sort of way—and that ache scared her more than all of Max's disapproving glances, dire warnings and fake statistics.

Max jumped up. "Sarah and I were just having a little chat, that's all."

Logan came straight for her, stopping at the other end of the sofa. He gazed down at her with concern. "Whatever he said, don't believe a word of it."

Sophia spotted him then, gave a happy giggle and waved her hands. "Hey there, beautiful." He dropped to the sofa on the other side of the carrier and scooped her up against his broad chest.

"Ga, dah," she said and grabbed for his nose.

"Well." Max stared at the man and the baby. Sarah couldn't tell if he looked bemused—or crestfallen. "I'll leave you alone. Wonderful to see you, Sarah."

She forced a nod and a smile. "See you later, Max."

Logan shook his head as Max disappeared through the dining room and out the door to the kitchen. "What did he say?"

Sarah rose and picked up the empty carrier. "It doesn't matter."

"If he's upset you—"

"Logan, I'm not upset." It was true. She was pretty much over Max and his issues with her as a potential bride for his oldest son.

She *wasn't* a potential bride—not for Logan or anyone. And Max had done her no harm.

In fact, their little chat had been a good thing. It had served to remind her that she was single and planned on staying that way. She liked Logan—maybe too much. He was kind and so generous. He made her laugh and she loved being with him. And whenever he kissed her, she wanted him to kiss her again, to keep kissing her and touching her and doing all those wonderful things to her that made her feel desired and satisfied in all the best ways.

But he wouldn't break her heart. She wouldn't let him. What they had together was no lifetime commitment. She wasn't counting on anything. They were both having a wonderful time for as long as it lasted.

And, she promised herself, she was perfectly happy with that.

Logan kind of had a bad feeling about whatever had gone down between his dad and Sarah while he was in the shower.

But Sarah insisted it was nothing, so he didn't pressure her to share the gory details. Max wasn't going to change and if she'd come to grips with that and decided not to let the old man bother her, that was all to the good. He had plans for the afternoon and he felt relieved that his dad hadn't ruined Sarah's mood.

Logan had packed a simple picnic, with sandwiches, chips and dip, a bottle of wine and cookies from Daisy's for dessert. It was gorgeous out, with the temperature in the high seventies, not too much wind and the sky a pure, cloudless blue.

Sarah carried the basket of food. He took the baby, the diaper bag and the picnic blanket. They strolled along the dirt road past the barn and the horse pasture to a spot he'd chosen under the dappled shade of an old bur oak.

"It's pretty here," she remarked approvingly. They spread the blanket. He put Sophia down on it and Sarah gave her a toy to chew on. The baby made her happy nonsense sounds and stared up through the branches. She even managed to roll over and push up on her hands a couple of times.

He poured them wine in paper cups and they ate. When Sophia got fussy, Sarah gave her a bottle and they took turns helping her hold it. Sophia was getting better at controlling her own bottle every day, it seemed to him. She also had two teeth coming in on the bottom in front. He could see the white rims peeking out of her gums whenever she gave him one of her giant smiles.

Kids. Logan had never seen himself as a guy who wanted children—no more than he'd ever thought he might get married.

But now he'd met Sophia. And lately, kids seemed like a pretty good idea to him.

And marriage? Well, he was kind of changing his opinion on that, too. The more time he spent with Sarah, the more he started thinking that he wouldn't mind being married at all.

He even *wanted* to be married.

As long as he could claim Sarah as his bride.

He had that urge to go for it—right then and there. The urge to pop the question now, as they sat beneath the old oak eating their cookies, watching Sophia hold her own bottle. He wanted to grab Sarah's hand and tell her exactly how he felt about her, what he wanted with her. To say how good forever sounded as long as he could share it with her.

But then he tried to remember that she'd had a rough time of it, and she wasn't all that trusting when it came to the male species. He felt that he *knew* her, that he understood her in all the ways that really mattered. Sometimes, in the past few days, he kind of forgot that he hadn't known her all his life.

He had to keep reminding himself that they hadn't been together for any length of time at all— just a week and a day. No way that was long enough for her to come to trust him. Any sudden moves involving emotional intimacy could scare her right off.

He didn't blame her for being commitment-shy.

That guy she'd lived with, Tuck Evans, was just a stone idiot. Logan wouldn't mind meeting that fool out behind the local cowboy bar, the Ace in the Hole, and going a few rounds with him. Then he'd thank him for blowing it royally and giving Logan a chance to have Sarah for his own.

As for that Mercer dude, Logan wouldn't mind doing a lot worse than beating him up. That guy had cheated on his wife *and* turned his back on Sophia. There were no words bad enough for someone like that.

Their loss, my gain, Logan reminded himself.

"Got a little surprise for Sophia," he said, as they were packing up the remains of their picnic.

Sarah gave him the side-eye. "I get nervous when you talk like that."

He leaned toward her, pulling her close and claiming her sweet lips in a slow, lazy kiss. Sophia, on the blanket between them, giggled up at them and crowed, "Ah, da, ga!"

Logan ran the backs of his fingers down Sarah's velvety cheek. *This is happiness. Who knew?* "Come on. You're going to love it." He kissed her again, because once was never enough.

She picked up the baby. He pulled his phone from his pocket and zipped off a quick text to Xander.

Bring Petunia. Now.

"What was that about?" Sarah watched him suspiciously as he put on his hat, tossed the blanket over his shoulder and grabbed the empty carrier, the basket and the diaper bag.

"I told you. It's a surprise." He started back toward the house.

She straightened Sophia's little sun hat and fell in

step beside him. "Okay, I know you're up to something and I know that it's something I'm not going to like."

He chuckled. "Now, what kind of attitude is that?"

"The attitude of a woman who's seen the way you operate, Logan Crawford."

"You've got it all wrong."

"You're trying to tell me you're *not* up to something?" She was just too cute.

He would have thrown an arm around her if he didn't have his hands full of all the stuff they'd carried out there. "No."

She frowned. "So you're admitting that you are up to something?"

"That's right, I am—and like I said, you're gonna love it."

Right then, Xander appeared from behind the barn leading a palomino pony.

Sarah could not believe her eyes. "Oh, you didn't."

Logan beamed. "He's a rescue. A Shetland. Just ten hands high, about eight years old with a really sweet disposition. I can't wait to see her ride him."

Sarah stopped in her tracks. "Her? You mean Sophia? Logan, she'll be six months old next week. That's way too young to be riding a pony."

He stopped, too. At least he had the grace to look a little sheepish now. "Okay. I know she's too young. What I meant to say was, I can't wait to see her ride him *when* she's old enough."

When she's old enough...

Those words just made it all worse somehow.

Sophia wouldn't be old enough to ride that pony for years.

Years.

Sarah couldn't take on the cost and commitment of caring for a pony in the hopes that someday her little girl might want to ride him. And she couldn't accept the pony as a gift for Sophia and expect Logan to keep him here at the Ambling A for her.

She and Logan, well, they didn't *have* years. That had been brought sharply home to her not two hours ago, thanks to Logan's own father. The point was to enjoy every moment, live completely in the now and not expect anything. Not to start making starry-eyed plans for some lovely, coupled-up future.

Sarah had spent her whole life looking ahead. She'd planned and schemed and set goals and kept her eyes on the prize of a great career, a successful marriage—kids eventually, after she made partner and could afford really good childcare.

And what had she gotten for all her "looking ahead"?

Nothing she'd planned on, that was for certain.

"Sarah." Logan dropped everything right there at his feet in the road. He stepped over the picnic basket and moved in close, pulling her and Sophia toward him, wrapping his strong arms around both of them.

With a long sigh, she let her body sway against him.

Oh, it felt good, so very good, to lean on him.

But she really couldn't afford to lean on a man, to get her hopes up that she could trust him, that she could count on him—and take the chance of having those hopes crushed to bits. She'd had her hopes crushed way more than enough already, thank you.

"Hey," he whispered. "It's okay. I promise. If you don't want her to ride Petunia, she won't ride Petunia." Snuggled in between the two of them, Sophia cooed in contentment. Logan tipped Sarah's chin up. "I get it. I do. I didn't mean to scare you. Petunia needed a home and so I took him and I couldn't help thinking that someday he might be just right for Sophia. But that's all. It was just a thought and it doesn't have to mean anything, I promise. It's nothing on you. *I* took the pony and I am responsible for him."

She sucked in a deep breath and her racing heart slowed down a little. Out of the corner of her eye, she saw Xander about twenty yards away. He'd stopped in his tracks. Smart man. The pony waited right behind him, patiently nibbling the weeds that grew in the center of the dirt road.

Logan pressed his forehead to hers. "You all right?"

"Yeah. I, um, overreacted. Somewhat. I guess."

He pulled back enough that their eyes could meet. "Somewhat?" One corner of that beautiful mouth lifted in a half smile that coaxed her to smile, too. "You freaked."

And then she did smile. "Yeah. I kind of did."

"But you're over that? You're okay?"

"I am, yeah." She thought how amazing he was. She wished she was someone else, someone still capable of really going for it, opening her heart, trusting that everything would work out all right in the end.

But she was just Sarah, strong enough to go on, yet cautious to a fault when it came to trusting a man again. Even a wonderful man who seemed to want to give her the world.

"And I have to ask…"

"What?"

"Petunia?" she taunted. "Seriously?"

"Hey. He was already named. I didn't want him to suffer an identity crisis on top of everything else."

She knew she shouldn't ask. "So...Petunia has had a difficult past?"

"He had mud fever and cracked heels from being left out in the open in bad weather. The vet's receptionist found him wandering around in the park. No owner ever showed up to claim him."

"How did they know his name was Petunia?"

"He was wearing a frayed bridle with Petunia tooled into the cheekpiece."

"Poor guy."

"Yeah. Dr. Smith treated him. When no owner appeared to take him home, he was offered for sale."

"And you took him."

"I like a survivor. Petunia is my kind of guy." He skated a finger down the bridge of her nose as Sophia let out another of her happy sounds. "How about I introduce you?"

"Sure."

He let her go. She resisted the urge to huddle close a little longer, make him hold her and her baby some more. Xander started forward again, the stocky little pony following right along behind him.

When Xander reached them, Sarah passed Sophia to Logan and petted the pony. Petunia stood placidly as she stroked his nose. When she smoothed his thick mane, he gave a friendly nicker. He really did seem like an amiable creature.

Logan teased, "I think he's going to be so happy living in the backyard at your place."

She groaned. "Don't even kid about it."

"Your loss. Wren's already in love with him."

"Good. I'm sure she'll take wonderful care of him."

The pony was so gentle and easy-natured that Sarah gave in and let Logan set Sophia on his back just for a moment. Logan held the baby steady and Xander moved in close to the animal, taking the lead right up under Petunia's chin with one hand, soothing him with the other.

Sophia waved her fists and bounced in Logan's hold, trusting completely the strong hands that supported her. Sarah might have choked up just a little at the sight. She bent and dug her phone out of the front pocket of the diaper bag and snapped a couple of pictures. What proud mama wouldn't?

Leaning close as he handed Sophia back to her, Logan whispered, "What'd I tell you? Sophia loves her new pony."

Her heart just melted. She gazed up at him adoringly and let herself imagine that they would stay together, that one of her baby's first words would be *Dada*, and when Sophia said it, she would be reaching for Logan.

For a brief and beautiful moment, Sarah knew it would happen.

But really, who was she kidding? Life was a challenge and things didn't always work out as a woman hoped they might.

She wouldn't start counting on anything. Expecting a magical happily-ever-after just wasn't wise.

Saturday was the painting party.

Logan and Sarah welcomed the same crew as the week before, and also two of Logan's brothers, Knox and

Hunter. Hunter brought Wren, who was a sweet girly-
girl. She carried Opal around with her and spent a lot
of time with Sophia, handing her teething toys, thrilled
to get a chance to give her a bottle.

With only two rooms to paint, they were finished
in the early afternoon. After cleanup, everyone hung
around to eat the wings and pizza Logan had ordered
and wandered out to sit on the front porch or to gather
under the big tree in the back.

Logan loved watching Sarah play hostess. She was
so conscientious. She made sure to visit with everyone,
to thank them for coming, to tell them how much she
appreciated the help.

Once all the guests had left, he and Sarah straightened up the place and put the dishes in the dishwasher.
Sophia was already asleep in her freshly painted room,
which had been tackled first so it would have plenty of
time to dry before her bedtime.

He and Sarah went to bed early and made slow, tender love.

Later, he held her as she slept and thought about all
the things he wanted to say to her. He wanted to talk
with her about the future—*their* future.

About where they might go, as a couple, from here.

No, they hadn't been together for that long. And she
was skittish about making any real plans with him. He
had a feeling his best move was *no* move, that he should
just let her be for a while, enjoy this time with her, give
her the space to come to fully trust him on her own.

But damn it, life was too short. Why waste a moment being cautious and careful when he knew what

he wanted, when he was certain that, deep in her heart, she wanted the same thing?

Yeah, all right. She'd been disappointed more than once. He got that. But he hadn't disappointed her so far, now had he? And he *wouldn't* disappoint her. He would be there for her and for Sophia. Whatever happened, she could depend on him, through the good times and the bad. He aimed to prove that to her.

Yeah, it was a little crazy, how gone he was on her. But he knew what he had with her. He didn't question it. He knew it was real. After all the years of never letting himself get too close to anyone, he finally wanted it all. With Sarah.

It kind of scared him how important she'd become to him—both her and Sophia—and so swiftly, too. But being scared didn't bother him. He found fear exhilarating. He would bust right through it, overcome it to claim what he wanted.

Sarah, though, held back. She guarded her heart. She just couldn't let herself trust him, not in the deepest way.

And he wanted everything with her. He wanted it now, wanted to break through the barriers she put up to protect herself, and show her she didn't need protection— not against him.

She stirred in his embrace.

He smoothed her tangled hair, wrapped his arms a little closer around her. She settled.

And he started thinking that hanging back, waiting for her to decide it was okay to trust him, was no solution. Action was called for.

He needed to make a real move. The move had to make a clear statement of his intent, of his purpose, of what he held for her in his heart. He needed to prove to her that he wasn't going anywhere. To show her that she was his and he was hers, and she didn't need to be afraid anymore.

He pulled the covers a little closer around them and closed his eyes. As sleep crept up on him, he smiled to himself.

It was really so simple. He knew what to do.

Chapter Ten

"Sarah?" her mom called as she came in the door of Falls Mountain Accounting early Monday morning.

"Be right there." She glanced down at Sophia, who was sound asleep in the carrier. The baby didn't stir. Sarah hurried into her office, put the carrier on the desk, set her laptop beside it and then let the diaper bag slide to the floor.

She went on to her dad's office, where her father leaned back in his leather swivel chair, looking happy and relaxed in a way he never had while she was growing up. Her mom, in a silky blouse, high heels and a pencil skirt, had hitched a leg up on the corner of his desk. Flo Turner looked downright sexy, kind of lounging there, eyes twinkling, grinning like the cat that got two bowls of cream.

Mack gave a low, gravelly chuckle. Flo leaned close to him and whispered something in his ear before turning her glowing smile on Sarah. "Come in and sit down, honey. We need to talk, the three of us, before we open for the day."

For no logical reason, Sarah felt a prickle of unease tighten the muscles at the back of her neck. But her parents seemed happy and totally in love as usual, so what was there to be anxious about?

She entered the room and took one of the guest chairs. "Everything okay?"

Her mom and dad exchanged another way-too-intimate glance, after which her dad said, "We have some big news and we felt it was time to share it with you."

Big news?

The craziest thought occurred to her: Could her mom be pregnant? Growing up, she'd longed for a little brother or sister.

Her mom was only forty-four. Sarah had read somewhere that there were women who didn't reach menopause until their sixties. Was her mom one of those?

If so, well…

A new brother or sister…?

Given the way her parents carried on lately, a new baby Turner didn't seem completely out of the realm of possibility.

The more she considered it, the more she liked the idea—loved it, even.

It would be great. Sophia's new aunt or uncle would be a year or so younger. They would grow up together, do all those things that siblings do. Fight and make up, keep each other's secrets and have each other's backs.

Life. It never ceased to amaze.

Her dad said, "Your mother and I are planning a big change."

"A move," Flo added, excited and so pleased as Sarah felt her big smile fading. "A move to the Gulf. We want to mix it up in a big way. Go where it's warm, live near the ocean."

What?

Wait.

Her mom and dad were moving, going miles and miles away?

No...

It couldn't be. Not now.

Not when she'd just come to realize how happy she was to have them nearby, to know she could turn to them whenever things got rocky. She'd let herself picture them helping her raise Sophia. She'd imagined how she would be there to support them as they grew old.

Yes, all right. There had been that initial shock of coming home to find her dried-up, depressing parents had fallen in love with each other and couldn't stop going at it right here in the office.

But in the past couple of weeks, she'd grown used to the way they were now, even come to like how open and loving they'd become with each other. She enjoyed being around them.

And now they were *leaving*?

They seemed oblivious to her distress. They grinned at each other, so pleased with their big plans. Mack said, "Fishing charters. That's what we're thinking. But first, we'll find a nice little place, get settled in, take it easy, you know, just your mother and me."

Flo leaned toward Mack again. She touched his face, a tender caress. "Your dad never wanted to be an accountant. Did you know that, sweetheart? This was your grandfather's office and it was always just assumed that Mack would enter the family business."

"I had hopes I would maybe try something different," Sarah's dad said gruffly. "I wanted a job where I could work outdoors."

"But then I got pregnant with you," said her mother. "We had to be responsible. And we were."

"So responsible," her dad echoed sadly, the lines in his face etching deeper as the corners of his mouth turned down.

"And I know, I know, we've spoken of all of this, of the bleak years." Her mom looked sad, too, for a moment. But then she brightened right up again. "What matters is that those days are behind us. You turned out amazing—our baby, all grown up now, with a baby of your own, so capable and smart, taking care of yourself and doing a great job of it. Your father and I feel it's okay now for us to move on, to make a change."

Mack caught Flo's hand and pressed his lips to it. "We're going to live the life we've both been longing for."

"At last." Her mom turned to beam at her again. "Honey, the office will be yours."

"And there's plenty of money," said her dad.

Flo laughed. "My parents and your Turner grandparents were big savers. We inherited a lot. And the business has done well. All these years, we never spent a penny we didn't have to spend."

"And we've invested wisely," added Mack.

"We have a hefty retirement," Flo said, "so we're all set. The cottage, our house, the business and a nice chunk of cash will all be yours. You'll have no problem hiring an office manager—and another accountant, if you think that's the way to go. And I know you've been resisting day care, but Just Us Kids is right here in town and it's excellent. They take babies. And you can definitely afford it, so just consider that, won't you?" Before Sarah could speak, she continued right on. "Of course, we plan to return often to be with you and our darling Sophia."

"However..." Mack sat forward in his chair and braced his forearms on the desk. "We *have* been thinking about Chicago."

"Yes," Flo chimed in. "We mustn't forget Chicago."

Sarah had no idea what they were talking about now. "Uh. We mustn't?"

Her mom plunked her hand over her heart. "Honey, when you decided to come home to live, we did offer to pitch in so that you could keep your high-powered job and your life in the city. You refused to take our money."

"Mom. You'd already put me through college. You paid for everything my scholarship didn't cover. I've got a degree from Northwestern and I have no loans to repay. It was enough. More than enough."

Her mom made a tutting sound. "Having Sophia was just such a challenge, we understood that. What I'm saying is, we probably should have pushed you harder to take what we offered and keep on with your original plans—and since then, it has occurred to us that maybe what you really want is to return to your life in Chicago. But you insisted on coming home and, well, of course we do love that you're here."

"We should have questioned you further as to what course you really wanted." Mack frowned regretfully. "But we didn't. And that's why we're offering again now. If you want that big-city life you always yearned for when you were growing up, we want you to have it. There should be more than enough money, especially if you sell the properties and the business, for you to make that happen comfortably, without all the stress and pressure you were under before."

"Whatever your dream is, you will be living it," said Flo. "I admit, it has seemed to me that you're making a good life for yourself here. And things do appear to be going so well with you and Logan…"

"But we realize," Mack jumped in, "that we might only be hoping you're happy here because Rust Creek Falls is our hometown and of course we would love to return here whenever the mood strikes and have you and our granddaughter right here waiting for us."

"That's simply not fair," said her mom. "We can just as well come and visit you and Sophia in Chicago. So we want you to know that however you choose to go forward, we will support you one hundred percent."

"Absolutely," Mack agreed. "Whatever you want to do next, we will help make it happen."

Both of them stared at her expectantly.

Sarah realized they were waiting for her to say something.

Well, she had plenty to say. Yeah, okay. They were being sweet and understanding and so very generous.

But it didn't matter.

She wanted to yell at them that their plans were utterly foolish, wildly irresponsible, to argue that they had no right to go pulling up stakes and running off to the Gulf, because…fishing charters? Seriously?

She wanted to beg them to change their minds and stay.

But none of those reactions would be right or fair or kind of her.

In all those unhappy years while she was growing up, she wasn't the only one who'd suffered. Her parents had suffered, too, locked into what they saw as their duty, every day gray and uninspired, a challenge to get through.

And now they'd changed everything. They'd found their happiness. And they had a dream they longed to pursue. She got that, about having dreams—even if her own dreams hadn't turned out the way she'd planned.

Their dreams were all new and shiny. And she wanted them to have those dreams. She wanted them to have it all.

"Honey?" Her mom was starting to look worried now.

"Just tell us," said her dad, "if there's something we're missing. If you have objections, we want to know."

"No." She gave them her brightest smile. "No objections."

"You're sure?" asked her mother.

"I am positive." Surprisingly, she sounded convincing even to her own ears. "And I'm happy for you two. I really am." Well, at least that was true. She was so glad for them, for what they'd found together after all these years. If only she and Logan might…

No. Really, she was fine on her own. *Better* on her own. It just didn't work for her, to go counting on a man, to start hoping for what wasn't meant to be.

Sometimes she worried that she might be getting too attached to him, that she shouldn't let him spend so much time with Sophia, who might suffer when the relationship ended. Really, though, he was so good with her.

And why would Sophia suffer if Logan left? She was just a baby, after all. Sophia required a steady, loving presence in her life, someone to count on now and all through her growing-up years. Other people—Sophia's father, her grandparents, Sarah's boyfriend, neighbors, babysitters—everyone else might come and go. But Sarah would be there for Sophia, always.

As for herself and her own relationship with Logan, well, maybe she was getting in too deep. Maybe she needed to think about having a talk with him, reminding them both that they shouldn't get serious, that this was just for now and it was absolutely perfect and not everything had to turn into a lifetime of love.

But oh, it did *feel* serious. And, well, she loved how serious it felt. She didn't really know what to do about that. Maybe they actually could have forever together.

Or maybe, once again, she was making plans for a future that would never come true.

What she needed was *not* to get all tied up in knots over her own current happiness with Logan. He was a good man and she would enjoy every moment they had together, with no expectations as to what might happen next.

"And Chicago?" asked her dad.

She shook herself and focused on the subject at hand. "No. I don't want to go back, I really don't. I'm staying here."

"Sweetheart…" Her mom jumped off the desk and held out her arms.

Sarah rose. Her dad got up and joined them in a family hug. It was so bizarre, group-hugging with her parents, of all people. It made her feel loved and cherished—and lonely already that they would be leaving.

"When will you go?" she asked as they stepped apart.

"It's a process," said Mack.

"We're eager to get started." Her mom looked down-right starry-eyed. "We want to get moving on it right away."

"I completely understand."

"We're going to sign over the business and the properties and give you the money we talked about," Flo announced. "We were hoping we could all three go together to see Ben as soon as possible." Ben Dalton was the family's attorney. He had an office right in town. "We want to get everything in your name so you can start the transition—hire your office manager, whom I will be happy to train, and get you ready to run the business on your own. And then we're buying a motor home."

"We're flexible," her dad insisted. "We'll be here for you for as long as you need us."

Her mom practically glowed in her excitement—to be on the way south, to start living their great adventure. "However long it takes to get everything worked out, that's fine with us. The truth is you're carrying most of the workload here already. Falls Mountain Accounting *should* be yours, anyway."

"You're ten times the accountant I ever was," her dad said wryly. "You've been here a couple of months and you've already enlarged our client list, streamlined the office procedures and bolstered the bottom line."

"There will be our house to deal with, packing stuff up, clearing it out a little," her mom chattered on. "You might want to move to the bigger place and sell the cottage. Or rent it. Or sell the house and—"

"Flo." Mack wrapped an arm around her. When she glanced up at him, he brushed a kiss on her forehead. "None of that has to be decided today."

Her mom gazed at him adoringly. "Of course, darling. You're right." She gave Sarah a rueful glance. "Sorry, honey. I got carried away."

"No problem." Except for how much she would miss them and how sad and lost she felt at the prospect of them living so far away. "I promise to consider all the options carefully."

"We know you will, sweetheart. And as for your father and me, if possible, we're hoping to be on our way south sometime in August."

Quietly, Logan shut the door to Sophia's room.

In two steps, he reached the arch that led into the dining room. At the sight of Sarah, he hung back to enjoy the view. She sat on the sofa with Opal in her lap. Even all the way across the room, he could hear that kitten purring.

Sarah scratched Opal's chin and the purring got louder. "What are you looking at?" she asked without glancing up.

"A pretty woman and a dinky white motorboat of a cat."

That got him a grin. "She's a happy baby."

He wanted to linger there, leaning on the door frame, just looking at her. And he also had the urge to go and get the spiral notebook from the kitchen. He wanted to capture the way her slim, pretty hands stroked Opal's soft, white fur.

Most of all, he wanted to go to her, sit beside her, put his arm around her and steal a kiss.

The prospect of getting close won out. He crossed the room, sat down next to her and drew her nice and snug against his side.

When she glanced up, he took her mouth.

It never got old, kissing Sarah. She smelled like heaven and she tasted even better. He nipped at her upper lip. She let out a sigh and he deepened the kiss—for a moment.

Not too long. If he kept kissing her, he would want more than kisses.

But a little later for that.

He lifted away and gazed down at her. "Something on your mind?"

A tiny frown marred the smooth skin of her forehead. She confessed, "Got some big news from the parents today. They're leaving everything—this house, their house, the business—to me and moving to the Gulf of Mexico."

"Wow."

A chuckle escaped her. It wasn't a very happy sound. "No kidding."

"When?"

"As soon as possible. A month or so."

He ran a finger down the side of her throat and then couldn't resist bending close again, sticking out his tongue, tasting her there. She tasted so good, like everything he wanted, like hope and forever. "You don't want them to go." He breathed the words against her silky, fragrant skin.

She caught his face between her hands and pushed away enough that she could look in his eyes. "How did you know that?"

"Easy. You didn't tell me they were leaving until I asked. If you weren't conflicted about them going, you would have said something earlier."

She searched his face. "You're way too observant."

"I get a big thrill out of observing you." He moved in close again and kissed her soft cheek. "Did you ask them to consider staying here in town?"

"No. And I'm not going to, either." She idly stroked the hair at his temple with the tips of her fingers. He loved the feel of her hands on him. "They can't wait to be on their way. And I want them to have what they want. They did everything they were supposed to do for years. It's time they got their chance to be free."

"But what about you?"

"I'll get over myself, believe me. Sophia and I will be fine."

Sophia and I. He wasn't included. She and Sophia were a family of two.

He wanted his chance to hear her say that the *three* of them would be fine, to consider them a unit. A family. Together. And he intended to *make* his chance. The sooner the better. "Let's go out."

She shook her head, laughing. "Sophia's already in bed in case you didn't notice when you put her there."

"I mean tomorrow night or the next one. I'll bet Lily would watch her, or your mom."

She skated a finger along the line of his jaw and he realized he was happy in the best kind of way, all easy and comfortable inside his own skin, just to be sitting here on the sofa with Sarah, Opal purring away on her lap.

"I'll try my mom first," she said. "She loves looking after Sophia and she mentioned today that she hoped to get more time with her before she and my dad ride off into the sunset in the fancy new Winnebago they're planning on buying."

"So that's a yes?"

"Mmm-hmm. I'll check with her, find out which evening's best."

"It's not even eight. There's still time to call. Do it now so I can make the reservation."

"Let me guess." Those golden-brown eyes twinkled at him. "You know this great little restaurant in Kalispell…"

"That's right." He leaned in close again to nip his way up the side of her neck and then nibble her earlobe for good measure. "Dinner at Giordano's because it's *our* place, our Italian restaurant."

"'Our place' that we've never been to together," she teased.

"A mere oversight which we are about to remedy. And we'll go dancing afterward, though I'll admit I'm not sure where to go for dancing around here."

"Well, I know where to go. The Ace in the Hole."

He scoffed at that. "From what I've heard, the Ace is a

cowboy bar with peanut shells on the floor and country-western on the jukebox."

"That's right," she said. "When I was a little girl, I always wanted to go to the Ace. You know, have a burger, beg quarters from my parents and play the jukebox. But my parents never went out anywhere—not even for a burger at the Ace."

"You were deprived of an important cultural experience. Is that what you're telling me?"

"That's it exactly. And for some reason I still don't really understand, as I got a little older, I didn't just go there myself or drag Lily there. I was like that as a kid, serious and quiet. I had trouble getting out there and doing the things I longed to do. I kind of lived in the future, planning for college and my life in the big city where I would make everything come together, make all of my dreams finally come true." She looked so sad then. But before he could figure out what to do about that, she brightened. "But then it happened. I did get my chance."

"For a burger at the Ace?"

"That's right." She laughed, a low, husky sound, and her eyes turned more golden than brown as she explained, "I was seventeen, in my senior year of high school and one of the Dalton boys invited me to go."

He wasn't sure he liked that faraway look she had. "Should I be jealous? Which Dalton boy?"

"No, you shouldn't. And which one doesn't matter. He never asked me out again."

"Good," he said gruffly, followed up with a muttered, "What an idiot."

"My point, Logan, is that I loved it. Loved the Ace.

It was noisy and there was lots of laughter. Music was playing and everyone was talking too loud. A couple of drunk cowboys even got in a fight, so there was excitement, too. There was everything I never had at home. I remember sitting there across from the Dalton boy whose first name you don't need to know and thinking that the Ace was the best and I wanted to come back every chance I got."

"And did you?"

She shook her head. "It just never happened. And then I left for Illinois in the fall."

"You haven't been there since that one date when you were seventeen, you mean?"

"That's right."

He captured her hand and kissed the tips of her fingers. "I'll take you."

She put her lips to his ear and whispered, "It can be *our* honky-tonk saloon where we make all our most precious romantic memories as we're two-stepping to country standards, peanut shells crunching underfoot. I take it you haven't been there even once yet?"

"Nope."

"Well, then, we're going to remedy that oversight after dinner at Giordano's."

"You're on." He tugged on her ponytail. "Are all accountants as romantic as you?"

"Nope." She kissed him, a quick press of her soft lips to his. "I'm special."

"Oh, yes, you are." He pulled her close and claimed a deeper, longer kiss, gathering her so tightly to him that Opal let out a tiny meow of annoyance at being jostled. The kitten jumped to the floor. When he lifted his head, Sarah's golden eyes were low and lazy, full of promise and desire. "Call your mom," he ordered gruffly. "Do it now."

Logan made the Giordano's reservation for seven Wednesday night. They got a quiet corner table, as he'd requested. He ordered a bottle of wine to go with the meal and the food was amazing as always. Even on a Wednesday night, most of the tables were full.

He hardly noticed the other customers, though. All his attention was on the beautiful bean counter across from him.

She wore a sleeveless turquoise dress, the sexy kind, with spaghetti straps. The dress clung to her curves on top. It had a flirty layered skirt that was going to swing out like the petals of a blooming flower later at the Ace when they danced together. Her gold-streaked brown hair was loose and wavy on her shapely bare shoulders.

He wanted to sketch her in that dress. And he would later, back at her cottage, when they were alone. If he got too eager to get her out of that dress, well, he would sketch it from memory as soon as he had the chance.

More than once during dinner, he almost made his move. But the moment just never seemed quite right. They joked about which Rust Creek Falls bachelorette Viv Dalton had most recently set up with which of his brothers. They spoke of the new office manager she and her mom had just hired. Flo had started training the new employee that morning. They laughed about how the work out at the Ambling A seemed downright endless. The barn needed more repairs and the fence-building went on and on.

For dessert, they had the chocolate semifreddo again, same as that first night when he'd had their meal catered at her house. She joked that it was "their dessert" and now he could never have it with anyone else but her.

He raised his coffee cup to her. "You. Me. Semifreddo. Forever."

She gazed at him across the small table, her eyes so soft, her skin like cream, her lush mouth begging for his kiss.

It was the exact right moment.

But he decided to wait.

Was he maybe a little freaked out about how to do what he planned—and when? Was he putting way too much emphasis on finding just the right moment?

Maybe.

But he wanted it to be perfect. In future years, he wanted her to remember the moment with joy and admiration for how he'd picked just the right time.

It was almost nine when they left Giordano's. They got in his crew cab and he leaned across the console for a kiss.

And wouldn't you know? One kiss was never enough.

They ended up canoodling like a couple of sex-starved kids for the next half hour or so, steaming up the windows, hands all over each other. Like they didn't have a comfortable bed to go to in the privacy of her cottage.

She'd unbuttoned his shirt and he'd pulled the top of that pretty dress down and bared her gorgeous breasts before they stopped—and that was only because he whacked his elbow on the steering wheel and they both started laughing at the craziness of them going at it right there in his truck at the curb in front of Giordano's. Anybody might see what they were up to.

Probably some innocent passerby *had* seen.

He buttoned and tucked in his shirt and she pulled her dress back up, after which she flipped down the visor and combed her hair in the mirror on the back. She looked so tempting, tipping her head this way and that, smoothing the unruly strands. He couldn't stop himself from reaching for her again.

She allowed him one long, hot kiss—and then she put her hands on his chest and pushed enough to break the connection. "The Ace," she instructed sternly. And then a giggle escaped her, which kind of ruined the effect. "We need to get going. Now."

The Ace in the Hole was a rambling wooden structure on Sawmill Street with a big dirt parking lot behind it and a wide front porch where cowboys gathered to drink their beer away from the music, to talk about horses and spot the pretty women as they came up the steps to go in.

Beyond the double doors, there was the long bar, a row of booths, a stage and a dance floor surrounded by smaller tables.

Sarah gazed out across the dance floor. "So romantic." She leaned close and brushed a kiss against his cheek. "Thanks for bringing me." The way she looked at him right then, her big eyes gleaming, mouth soft with a tender smile—made him feel about ten feet tall.

He got them each a beer and they took a booth. Tonight, a local band had the stage. They played cover versions of familiar country songs.

"Let's dance," she said, smiling, a little flushed, her

eyes full of stars to be here at this cowboy bar where she hadn't been since she was seventeen.

They danced every song—fast ones and slow ones, never once returning to the booth.

The whole time, he was waiting as he'd been waiting all evening—for just the right moment. He might have done it there, on the dance floor of the cowboy bar she'd found so thrilling when she was a kid.

But no.

Private was better, he decided at last. He would wait until they got back to the cottage.

Around eleven, as they swayed together, their arms around each other, to Brad Paisley's "We Danced," she lifted her head from his shoulder and let out a giggle. She seemed thoroughly pleased with herself.

"What?" he demanded.

"Nothing—except it's official. I've danced at the Ace with the hottest guy in town. I never thought it would happen, but look at me now."

"You are so beautiful." Words did not do her justice. He dipped his head and kissed her, one of those kisses that starts out gentle and worshipful, but then kind of spins out of control.

She was the one who pulled away. "I'm thinking we probably ought to go soon," she whispered, sweetly breathless.

"I'm thinking you're right."

They left when the song ended.

At the cottage, Flo reported that Sophia had been an angel. "She had her bottle and ate her mashed peas and then some applesauce and went down at eight thirty. I haven't heard a peep from her since." They thanked her for babysitting.

Flo kissed Sarah's cheek. "Anytime," she said as she went out the door.

And finally, it was just Logan and Sarah, with the baby sound asleep. She scooped the snoozing Opal off the sofa and put her in her bed in the laundry room.

When she came back, he did what came naturally, pulling her into his arms and lowering his mouth to hers, walking her backward slowly as he kissed her.

In the bedroom, he almost guided her down to the bed.

But no. It was time.

Past time—to make his move. Say his piece. Ask her the most important question of all.

She gazed up at him, kind of bemused. Wondering. "What is it? There's something on your mind."

He took the ring from his pocket. She gasped. He was smiling as he dropped to one knee. "Sarah," he said.

And that was as far as he got.

Because she covered her mouth with her hands and cried, "No!"

Chapter Eleven

Logan felt as though she'd walloped him a good one—just drawn back her little fist and sent it flying in a roundhouse punch. He reeled. "What? Wait…"

"Logan. Get up. Don't do this, okay?" She actually offered him her hand, like he needed help to get up off the floor.

He rose without touching her and put the ring back in his pocket. He had no idea where this was going—except it was nowhere good, that was for sure.

She backed up until her knees touched the bed and then she kind of crumpled onto the edge of the mattress. He watched her hard-swallow. She didn't look well—her face was dead white with two spots of hectic color, one high on each cheek.

"Uh, sit down," she said and nervously patted the space beside her.

He shook his head. "I think I'll stand."

She stared up at him, begging him with her eyes—but for what? "I'm so sorry." She spoke in a ragged voice. "This isn't—I mean, I just can't, Logan. You're the most incredible man and I'm wild for you, you know I am. But I couldn't say yes to marriage. I just couldn't. Please try to understand. This thing with us, it's just for now and we both know that. We have to remember that."

"No." He shut his eyes, drew in a slow, careful breath. "No, I don't know that. I'm not going anywhere. Never. I want to be right here, with you."

"But it's not going to last. We're just, I mean, well, living in the moment, having fun, enjoying the ride. And it's beautiful, what we have together. Why ruin it with expectations that will break my heart and could hurt my daughter when they don't pan out?"

How could she think that? "You're wrong."

"No. I'm not wrong. I'm realistic. Nothing ever really does last, you know?"

"No, Sarah. I don't know." He also didn't know what to do next, how to reach her, how to recover from this. But then it came to him that he had to go all the way now, to say it out loud, to give her his truth. It was all that he had. "I love you, Sarah Turner. I want to marry you."

She let out another cry and clapped her hands to her ears this time. Her eyes glittered with moisture. A tear got away from her and carved a shining trail down her cheek.

He tried reassurance. "You don't have to be afraid. I'm not going to stop loving you. Not ever. This is for real. I swear it to you."

"You say that now—"

"Because it's true. Because what we have, what I feel for you, I've never felt before. I trust what we have. I love you. I love Sophia. I want to take care of you, of both of you. I want to be here when Sophia says her first real word, when she takes her first step. I want to be here for all the days we're given, you and me. This is where I'm happy. This is where it all makes sense. With you, with Sophia. The three of us. A family."

"I can't," she said again. "I just can't. I can't do that. It's one thing for us to take it a day at a time. To enjoy what we have while it lasts. But marriage? Logan, that's not what this is about."

"Yeah, it is."

"No. It's not." She said it so firmly, her shoulders drawn back now, her expression bleak, closed down.

He kept trying to reach her. "It's so simple. It's just you and me doing what people do when they love each other, starting to build a life together. Making it work."

"Your father hates me."

Really? She was going to go there? Patiently, he answered her, "No, he does not hate you. My mother broke his heart and ran off with her lover, abandoning him and me and my brothers. We never heard from her again."

She gasped. He saw sympathy in her eyes. "That's horrible."

"Yeah. It was pretty bad for all of us. And that's why he is the way he is. He's a lonely old man with some weird ideas about love and marriage. You're too smart to let Max Crawford chase you away."

"It's not only your dad. It's, well…" She blew out a breath, folded her hands and then twisted them in her lap. "Love just never works out for me."

"That's faulty reasoning, Sarah. You know it is. There was what? That idiot Tuck who didn't know the best thing that ever happened to him when he had it? Good riddance. And that Mercer guy? That wasn't love anyway, was it?"

Her eyes reproached him. "You're making fun of me."

"No, I'm not. I'm just saying that whatever you're really scared of, I don't think it's anything you've brought up so far."

"I, well, it's only… Logan, what if a year goes by and you realize you made a mistake?"

"That's not going to happen. I know what's in my heart. You're the one for me. That's never going to change."

"But, Logan, what if your feelings did change? What if we, you and me, didn't work out after a year or two or three? Think back. Try to remember how it was for you when your mother deserted you."

"I know exactly how it was, which is all the more reason I will never desert you."

She just couldn't believe him. "In a couple of years, Sophia will be old enough to suffer when you leave us."

"You're not listening. If you say yes to me, I will never leave you."

She only shook her head and went right on with her argument. "My daughter would count on you to be there and you would be gone. She would suffer because of my bad choices. It's just better not to go there. It's just better to leave things as they are."

He stood over her, burning to get closer, to reach down and take her hand, pull her up into his arms that ached to hold her. But she looked so fragile sitting there, as though his very touch would shatter her.

"I'm so sorry," she whispered on a broken husk of breath. "I'm so sorry but I can't. It's not possible. Not for me."

He didn't know how to answer her. Because words weren't making a damn bit of difference. He could stand here and argue with her all night long.

And where would that get them? What would that fix?

"Just tell me what you're really afraid of." He was actually pleading now. Imagine that. Logan Crawford, whose heart had always been untouchable, pleading with a woman just for a chance. "I can't fix this if I don't know what's broken."

"But that's it," she cried. "It's nothing you can fix. Nothing anyone can fix. I can't let myself count on you—on anyone, not really. I have to look out for my daughter and my heart. I have to be strong, be the mom and the breadwinner, the decision-maker and the protector, too. I don't have the trust in me to let someone else do any of that, not anymore. It doesn't matter how I feel about you, or how much I care. If I can't give my trust, well, it's not going to work."

Trust. There it was. The thing she feared to give. The real problem.

She couldn't—*wouldn't*—allow herself to trust in him.

How the hell was he supposed to break through something like that?

What a spectacular irony. He'd finally found the one

woman he wanted to spend a lifetime with. And she couldn't let herself believe in him.

Where did that leave them?

His heart felt so empty, hollowed out. What now?

Should he back off, forget about forever and try to convince her to simply go on as they were?

Really, it was so achingly clear to him now: he'd messed up. Jumped the gun, made his move too soon. He should have kept his damn mouth shut, not crossed this particular line until she'd had more time to see that it was safe to believe in him.

He'd rushed it. He got that.

And it really didn't look like there was any way for him to recover from this disaster.

Shoving his hands in his pockets, he made a last-ditch attempt to salvage some small shred of hope. "So then, I have to know. I want you to tell me. Is it that you need more time?"

She gazed up at him, a desolate look on her unforgettable face. "No." The single word came at him like a knife blade, shining and deadly, flying straight for his heart.

He made himself clarify. "Never. You're saying never."

She nodded and whispered, "I am so sorry."

Well, okay. That was about as clear as it could get. She hadn't hedged. She'd given him zero hope that he could ever change her mind.

And now she was watching his face, reading him. "You're leaving," she said.

Before he could answer, the baby monitor on the dresser erupted with a sharp little cry.

They both froze, waiting for Sophia to fuss a little and then go back to sleep.

Not this time, though. Sophia cried out again. And again. Each cry was more insistent.

Sarah started to rise.

"I'll get her," he said.

"No, really, it's—"

He cut her off. "Let me tell her goodbye. Give me that, at least."

She pressed her lips together and dipped her head in a nod.

He turned for the baby's room.

Sarah watched him go.

Dear Lord, what was the matter with her? She loved him. She did. And he'd never been anything but trustworthy with her, with Sophia.

And yet, she just couldn't do it, couldn't put her future in his hands, couldn't let herself believe that he would never break her heart, never change his mind after she'd given him everything, never turn his back on her and her child.

Sophia's wailing stopped.

Sarah heard Logan's voice, a little muffled from the other room, but crystal clear on the monitor. "Hey there, gorgeous. It's all right. I've got you. I'm right here."

The camera had come on. It used infrared technology so that even in Sophia's darkened room, she could see the tall figure standing by the crib with her baby in his arms.

"Ah, da!" cried Sophia. With a heavy sigh, she laid her head against Logan's chest. "Da..."

"I think we've got a wet diaper here, don't we?"

"Unngh."

The camera tracked him as he carried Sophia to the changing area. Handing her a giraffe teething ring to chew on, he quickly and expertly put on a fresh diaper. "There now. All better."

"Pa. Da." Clutching the ring in one tiny fist, she reached out her arms to him.

He scooped her up against his chest again and carried her to the rocker in the corner. "We'll just sit here and rock a little while, okay?"

"Angh." She stuck the teething ring in her mouth.

He cradled her in both arms and slowly rocked. "I wanted to talk to you, anyway." The baby sighed and stared up at him. "Sophia, I have to go now. I am so sorry, but I won't be back. I want you to know, though, that I would stay if I could. I would be your 'da' forever and ever. I would watch you grow up, teach you how to ride a bike and how to pitch a softball, help you with your homework, chase all the boys away until the right one came along..."

Sarah's eyes blurred with tears. On the monitor, Sophia gazed up at Logan so solemnly, as though she understood every word he said.

He fell silent. For a while, he just cradled her, rocking, looking down at her as she stared up at him. Slowly, her eyes fluttered shut. She let go of the toy. He caught it and set it on the little table beside the rocker.

Several more minutes passed. In her bedroom, Sarah watched on the monitor as Logan bent close to brush the lightest of kisses across her daughter's forehead.

He whispered something more, but she couldn't make out the words.

And then, moving slowly so as not to disturb the little girl in his arms, he rose and carried her to the crib. Carefully, he put her back down again, pulling the blanket up to tuck in gently around her. He leaned down for a last light kiss.

A moment later, he came and stood in the open door to Sarah's room. "She's sleeping now. I'm going."

Sarah didn't know what else to do, so she got up and followed him to the front door. He pulled it open. The night air was cool, the dark street deserted.

He stuck his hand in his pocket. She looked down and saw he was holding out the house key she'd given him. She took it. "Goodbye, Sarah."

She wanted to reach for him, grab him close. She wanted to *not* let him go.

But she only stood there, the key clutched tight in her hand. She made herself say it. "Goodbye, Logan."

He turned, went out the door and down the steps to where his crew cab waited.

She couldn't bear to watch him drive away, so she shut the door and kind of fell back against it, her knees suddenly weak and wobbly. Outside, she heard the truck start up, pull away from the curb and head off down the street.

The big, black eye of his fancy TV stared at her disapprovingly. She should have given it back to him. That had been her plan when she allowed him to bring it here—to return it to him when their time together ended.

Sarah shut her eyes. A sound escaped her—something

midway between a crazy-woman laugh and a broken sob. As if the TV even mattered. If he wanted it, he would come back and get it.

But she knew he wouldn't. He would want her to have it.

And he wouldn't want to see her or talk to her.

Ever again.

Chapter Twelve

Somehow, Sarah got through the next day. And the next.

It wasn't easy. She had this horrible hollow feeling—like her heart had gone missing from her chest.

But she knew it had been the right thing to tell him no. To break it off. The longer she had with him, the more painful it would have been to lose him in the end.

She managed to avoid her parents for those first two days, taking all of her appointments away from the office, being too busy to talk when her mom called on Friday.

Friday night was really tough. Sophia was fussier than usual. It wasn't a cold or an ear infection or the pain of teething. Sarah thought the baby seemed sad. And Opal kind of drooped around the house like her little kitty heart was broken.

It couldn't be true that her baby *and* her kitten missed

Logan as much as she did. Sophia was too young to even know he'd gone missing—wasn't she? And Opal was a cat, for crying out loud. Cats got attached to their place, their surroundings. Plus, if Opal had a favorite human, it was Sarah, hands down. She'd been Sarah's cat from the first. The kitten sat in her lap while they watched TV and came crying to her when the kibble bowl was empty.

No. Sarah knew what was really going on. She was projecting her own misery and loss onto her baby and Opal. She needed to stop that right now. She'd done the right thing and this aching, endless emptiness inside her would go away.

Eventually.

That night after Sophia finally went to sleep, Sarah sat on the sofa with her phone in her hands and studied the pictures of Logan, Sophia and Petunia that she'd taken that day they had their picnic at the Ambling A. She went through the notebook of Logan's sketches. It hurt so much to look at them. She'd been planning to frame some of them and put them up around the cottage.

But she didn't know if she could ever bear to do that now. Those sketches were a testimony to all she would never have, all she'd made herself say no to.

All she had to learn to let go.

Saturday morning, her mom appeared on her doorstep. "Okay," said Flo. "What is going on with you?"

When Sarah tried to protest that she was fine, her mom kind of pushed her way in the door, shut it behind her, took Sophia right out of her arms and said, "Pour me some coffee. We need to talk."

They sat in the kitchen where the morning sun streamed cheerfully in the window above the sink and the walls were the beautiful, buttery yellow Sarah had chosen herself—and that Logan had made happen. Every wall in her house was now the color she wanted it to be.

Because of Logan. Because he'd kept after her until she finally agreed to the painting party—and then, when she did agree, he'd taken her out to buy the paint and then worked for two days painting and also supervising the volunteer crew.

If not for Logan, she'd still be living in a house with off-white walls and random brushstrokes of color here and there, promising herself that one of these days she would get around to making the place feel more like her home.

Flo put Sophia in her bouncy seat and gave her a set of fat, plastic keys to chew on. Then she sat at the table across from Sarah and took a sip of her coffee. "It's Logan, right?"

"Mom, I don't think we—"

"He's not here and he hasn't been for days."

"How do you know that?"

"Sweetheart, it's Rust Creek Falls. Everybody knows that. No one's seen that fancy pickup of his out in front since Wednesday night."

"Mom, I really don't want to talk about it."

"But you *need* to talk about it. Now, tell me what happened."

"I, um…" Her throat locked up, her nose started running and suddenly there were tears streaming down her cheeks. "Mom, he proposed. He proposed to me and I sent him away."

Flo got up again. She grabbed the box of tissues from over on the counter and set them in Sarah's lap, bending close to hug her right there in her chair. "Mop up, honey. We need to talk." Flo sat down again and sipped her coffee, waiting.

Sarah blew her nose and dried her cheeks.

"Tell me," her mom demanded.

With a big sigh and another sad little sob, Sarah started talking. She told her mom pretty much everything, all about how beautiful and perfect Wednesday night had been—until Logan tried to propose.

Once she started talking, she couldn't stop. She spilled it all, about her disappointments with Tuck and the sheer rat-crappiness of Mercer Smalls, how she just couldn't trust a man anymore and so she knew it was the best thing, to end it with Logan now.

When she finally fell silent, she glanced over and saw that Sophia had fallen asleep in her bouncy chair, her little head drooping to the side, the plastic keys fallen to the floor, where Opal batted at them and then jumped back when they skittered across the tile.

Her mom got up and poured them each more coffee, put the pot back on the warmer and then resumed her seat. "Before we get into everything you've just told me, I have to ask. Are you upset over your dad and me leaving? Is that bothering you? Do you want us to stay?"

Sarah opened her mouth to insist that she didn't, no way, no how.

But before she got the words out, her mom shook her head. "Tell me the truth, honey. Please."

Sarah dabbed at her eyes to mop up the last of her tears. "Okay, it's a factor, that you're going. I will miss you. I mean, all those years growing up, it was like we were strangers sharing a house. And now, it's so different. You and Dad are helpful and fun. You've become the parents I always wished for and it's been so great having you nearby. But no. I don't want you to stay. If you stayed, you wouldn't be getting your dream and I want that, Mom. I want you and Dad to finally live the life you never let yourselves live before."

"But if you need us—"

"You're a phone call away. If I needed you, you would be back in a flash."

"But do you need us to *be* here, day-to-day? Do you need us close by?"

Sarah leaned forward and took her mom's hand between both of hers. "No. You and Dad are going. It's settled. I'm good with it, I promise you."

Her mom pulled her hand free of Sarah's hold, only to reach out and fondly smooth Sarah's hair. "And what about *your* dream, sweetheart?"

"Um. Yeah, well. That's life, you know."

Flo let out a wry laugh. "Honey, you grew up a lonely child in a silent house with unhappy parents. Then you set out to conquer Chicago. You worked so hard, got so far. But sometimes in life, our big plans don't turn out the way we want them to. You had to come home. I know it hasn't been easy for you, with so much on your shoulders. But the past few weeks, you've seemed to thrive. You're really good at running the business. I think you've been happy, especially since you've been with Logan. You've been sprucing up the cottage, settling in beautifully here with a little help from your friends and neighbors. It seems to me you've been having a pretty fine time in your old hometown."

Sarah sat back in her chair and eyed her mother warily. "You've become so upbeat and hopeful. Sometimes it's just exhausting."

Her mother laughed some more. "Well, honey, now think about. Ask yourself, is it maybe just possible that you came home in defeat only to discover that you can have your dream here? Is it possible that taking over the family business is more satisfying work for you than killing yourself at that giant firm in the big city? Is it possible you *like* running your own show, being your own boss? And as for Logan, well, the two of you seem to me like a great match. Didn't he offer you exactly what you've longed for—a good life with the right man, a father for your child?"

"Mom, it didn't work out, okay?"

"But it could." Flo leaned in again. "If you'll just let it."

Sarah glared at her. "Look. You want me to say it?"

Flo sat up straight again and smiled way too sweetly. "I do, yes. I absolutely do."

"Okay, Mom. I'll say it." Sarah sniffed and brushed another random tear away. "I freaked out. That's the truth. He went down on one knee to offer me just what I'd given up on, what I've always wanted most and have learned to accept that I'll never have. And when he pulled out that ring, well, I choked, okay? I just couldn't do it, couldn't reach out and take it." Sarah put her hands to the sides of her head because right at that moment it kind of felt like her brain was about to explode. "I blew it. I really did. I threw away my own dream. I turned away the man I love. I freaked out and now it's too late."

"Oh, sweetheart," said her mother. "As long you're still breathing, it's never too late."

Logan had taken to sleeping out under the stars.

After all, there were a lot of fences to fix on the Ambling A. He was taking care of that—and avoiding any contact with other human beings in the bargain.

The morning after it ended with Sarah, he'd had an argument with his father over nothing in particular. Really, he picked a fight because he blamed Max, at least partly, for the way it had all gone wrong with Sarah.

Then, that same day at breakfast, his brothers were yammering on about some discovery they'd made—an old, locked diary with a jewel-encrusted letter *A* on the front. They'd found it right there in the ranch house under a rotted floorboard and they were all trotting out theories as to who might have hidden it and what might be inside.

Logan could not have cared less about some old, tattered relic that had nothing to do with him or any of them, either. He yelled at them to shut the hell up about it.

Then Wilder made the mistake of asking him what his damn problem was. He'd lit into his youngest brother. They'd almost come to blows.

That did it. Logan realized he would just as soon not have anything to do with his family right now—or with anyone else, for that matter. He'd considered leaving for good, packing up his things and heading back to Seattle.

But the big city didn't thrill him any more than dealing with his family did. Nothing thrilled him. He was fresh out of enthusiasm for anything and everything. Until he could figure out what move to make next, he just wanted to be left alone.

So he'd loaded up his pickup with fence posts and barbwire and headed out across the land. He had a sleeping bag and plenty of canned food. For five full days he worked on the fences, brought in strays, dug out clogged ditches and didn't speak to a single person.

Eventually, he would have to return to the ranch house, have a hot meal, a bath and a shave. But not for a while yet. Not until he could look at his father without wanting to punch his lights out, not until his heart stopped aching.

Come to think of it, it could be a long time before he had a damn shower. Because the ache in his heart showed no signs of abating anytime soon.

On Tuesday, three days after her talk with her mother, Sarah had yet to do anything about how much she missed Logan.

Yeah, she got it. She did. She'd finally had a chance at what she really wanted with a man—and she'd thrown her chance away. It was up to her to go to him, tell him how totally she'd messed up and beg him to give her just one more shot.

But she didn't do it. She felt…immobilized somehow. She visited clients, cared for her baby, cuddled her cat. Inside, though, she was empty and frozen and so very sad.

Tuesday evening, as Opal jumped around the kitchen floor chasing shadows and Sophia sat chewing her rubber pretzel and giggling dreamily at the mobile of dancing ladybugs hooked to her bouncy seat, Sarah stood at the refrigerator with the door wide open.

She stared inside at food she had no interest in eating and tried to decide what to fix for dinner. Really, she wasn't hungry. There was a half a box of Cheez-Its on the counter. She could eat that—yeah. Perfect. Cheez-Its for dinner, and maybe a glass of wine or ten. Once she put Sophia to bed, she could cry for a while. That would be constructive.

The knock on the front door surprised her. Would it be her mom again or maybe Lily, somebody who loved her coming to tell her to snap out of it?

She almost didn't answer it. Really, she didn't want to talk to anyone right now and she couldn't figure out why anyone would want to give a pep talk to an emotional coward like her, anyway.

But then whoever it was knocked again. She shut the fridge door and went to get it.

"Hello, Sarah," Max Crawford said when she opened the door. He actually had his black hat in his hands. "I wonder if you would give me a few minutes of your time."

Her best option was obvious. She should slam the door in his overbearing, judgmental face.

Instead, she just sneered. "Didn't you get the memo? Logan and I broke up. You got what you wanted. There is absolutely no reason for you to be darkening my door."

"Please," he said, all somber and serious—and way too sincere. "A few minutes, that's all I'm asking for. Just hear me out."

Oh, she wanted to shove that door shut so fast and so hard…

But she didn't. Partly because she was too tired and sad to give him the angry, self-righteous rejection he deserved. And also because she couldn't help but be curious as to what Logan's rapscallion dad had to say now.

She stepped back and gestured him inside. "Have a seat."

He crossed the threshold and sat on the sofa. "Thank you."

She took the easy chair across from him. "Okay. What?"

Carefully, he set his hat on the cushion beside him. "Logan's out on the far reaches of the Ambling A. He took a sleeping bag, a truck-bed full of barbwire and fence posts, a shovel or two and a bunch of canned goods. He hasn't been back to the house since last Thursday."

Alarm had her heart racing and her palms going sweaty. "You're saying he's disappeared?"

"No, he's mending fences and bringing in strays. We been out, me and the boys, checking on him from a distance because he wants nothing to do with any of us. Sarah, you broke my boy's heart."

She saw red. She would have raised her voice good and loud, given him a very large piece of her mind, if it hadn't been for the innocent baby in the other room who would be frightened if her mother started screaming like a crazy woman.

With deadly softness, she reminded him, "Well, I guess you're pretty happy then, since that was what you wanted all along."

"I was wrong," said Max. "I was all wrong."

That set her back a little. She blinked and stared. "What did you say?"

"I just need you to know that I am so sorry, Sarah, for any trouble I have caused between you and Logan. I truly apologize for my behavior. I'm a guilty old man with too many secrets. I see—and I always saw—that you are a fine woman. And my son does love you. He loves you so much. I get it now, I do. Trying to chase you off was wrong. I never should have done that, and that I did it had nothing to do with you. It was a knee-jerk reaction born of my own bad deeds in the past."

Okay, now she was really curious. "Exactly what bad deeds, Max?"

He picked up his hat and tapped it on his knee. "Well, Sarah, at this time, I'm not at liberty to say."

She snort-laughed at that one. "Of course, you're not."

He had the nerve to chuckle. "Sarah, I just want you to know that I am finished trying to come between you and Logan. When you two work it out, I will be there for both of you, supporting you in every way I can."

"*When* we work it out?"

"That's what I said."

"You have no way of knowing that we will work it out."

"My son is long-gone in love with you. His heart may be broken, but he has not given up on you. He's just licking his wounds for a while, until he's ready to try again." Max rose. "He took his phone with him when he left, so if you were to call in order to put him out of his misery, chances are you would get through." He went to the door.

She followed him—until he stopped suddenly and turned back to face her. For several seconds they just stood there, regarding each other.

Sarah broke the silence. "You know where he is, right? You could take me to him?"

"Yes, ma'am."

"I'll be at the Ambling A ranch house at eight tomorrow morning."

The lines around Max's eyes deepened with his devilish grin. "Now that is what I was hoping you might say."

Sarah decided against Cheez-Its and wine for dinner— not because she knew she should eat something more substantial, but because she was so nervous about what might happen tomorrow that she couldn't eat at all.

She fed Sophia, gave her a bath and put her down to sleep at a little after eight. Then she sat in the living room with a pencil and a scratch pad trying to organize her thoughts for tomorrow. She wanted to have something really meaningful and persuasive to say when she finally saw Logan again, something to convince him that she truly did love him, that he could trust her with his heart. She needed just the right words, words that would reassure him, make him believe that if he said yes to her, she would not disappoint him ever again.

It was almost nine when she heard the truck pull up out in front.

An odd little shiver went through her and she rose to peer out the window behind the sofa.

It was Logan's crew cab, all covered in dust and dried mud, with a big roll of barbwire sticking up out of the bed.

With a cry, she threw down the scratch pad and ran to the door, flinging it open just as he got out of the truck. She stepped out on the porch and then kind of froze there as his long strides took him around the front of the truck and up the front walk.

He looked so good, in a nice, blue shirt and dark-wash jeans, clean-shaven, his hair still damp. He must have come in from the wild, talked to his dad, had a shower and a shave.

Her heart was going so fast she kind of worried it might beat its way right out of her chest, just go jittering off up Pine Street and vanish forever from her sight.

He stopped at the foot of the steps. "Sarah," he said. That was it. That was everything. Really, how did he do it? He could put a whole world of meaning into just saying her name.

"Yes," she said.

"Sarah." And he came up the steps.

"Yes!" She threw herself into his waiting arms. "All the yeses. All the time. Forever, Logan. I'm sorry I was so scared. I'm sorry I blew it. I choked in the worst kind of way. But I'm over that. I want a life with you. I want our forever. I want it, I do."

His Adam's apple bounced as he gulped. "You mean that?" His eyes gleamed down at her, full of hope and promise and so much love.

"I do. Oh, yes, I do. I love you, Logan. I've missed you so much. If you give me one more chance now, I will never let you down again."

"Yeah," he said, one side of that fine mouth quirking up in a pleased smile. "That's what I'm talking about." And he kissed her, a long kiss, full of all the glory and wonder and desire she'd been missing so desperately since she sent him away.

She melted into him, happier than she'd ever been in her whole life up till now.

And when he lifted his head he said, "Give me your hand." He pulled the ring from his pocket and slipped it on.

"It's so beautiful." And it was, emerald-cut with smaller diamonds along the gleaming platinum band. "I love it." She cast her gaze up to him again. "I love *you*."

"And I love you. So much. Sarah..." He grabbed her close for another kiss and another after that.

Then someone whistled. They looked out at the street to see one of the neighborhood kids jumping on his bike, speeding off, laughing as he went.

Sarah caught Logan's hand and pulled him inside. He shoved the door shut and grabbed her close again.

She said, "Your dad came to see me today."

"I know. He told me."

"I was coming after you tomorrow."

"He told me that, too. I couldn't wait. So here I am."

She lifted a hand and pressed it to his warm, freshly shaven cheek. "Oh, I am so glad. I want to—"

A cry from the monitor on the coffee table cut her off.

"I'll go get her," said Logan. They shared a long look. He knew the drill, after all. If they just waited, the baby might go back to sleep. "I need to see her," he said. "I need to tell her I'm here now and I'm not going away again."

Sarah blinked back happy tears. "Yeah. Go ahead."

Logan yanked her close and kissed her hard—and then turned for the short hall to the baby's room.

"Reow?" Opal sat beneath the dining room table. Delicately, she lifted a paw and spent a moment grooming it. Then she stretched and strutted over to where Sarah stood by the door.

Sarah scooped her up and kissed her on the crown of her head between her two perfect pink ears. "Logan's home," she whispered.

Opal started purring.

In the baby's room, Logan turned the lamp on low and went to the crib.

Sophia let out the sweetest sound at the sight of him—something midway between a laugh and a cry. She waved her hands wildly. "Ah!" she crowed. "Da!"

"How's my favorite baby girl?" he asked as he gathered her into his arms.

Much later, in bed after a more intimate reunion, Logan and Sarah made plans.

They would live in town—at the cottage for now, and eventually in the larger house where she'd grown up. Before they moved, Logan was going to get that garage-door opener installed and hire some guys to build the breezeway from the garage to the back door. They would keep the cottage for Flo and Mack so they would have their own place in their hometown any time they wanted a break from their adventures in the Gulf.

Neither Logan nor Sarah wanted to wait to get married. Her parents would be leaving soon and Sarah insisted the wedding had to happen before they headed south.

"How about Monday?" she suggested.

He blinked at her in surprise. "Monday as in a week from yesterday?"

"Yep. That's the one. We'll get the license tomorrow and I'll call Viv, explain what I want and see if she can make it happen."

"Sarah, don't most brides take months, even a year, to plan a wedding?"

She laughed and kissed him. "They do, but Viv Dalton is a miracle worker. Just you wait and see."

Epilogue

The following Monday at six in the evening, Mack Turner walked Sarah down the aisle Viv had created within a magical cascade of fairy lights in the center of the dance floor at the Ace in the Hole.

Monday, after all, was relatively quiet at the Ace and that meant the owner had been willing to close for a wedding—but really, since everyone in town was invited and most of them showed up, the Ace wasn't closed at all. The place was packed.

The tables were decked out in yellow-and-white checkered cloths with wildflower centerpieces and candles shimmering in mercury glass holders. Sarah wore a floor-length strapless lace gown that she and Lily had found in a Kalispell wedding boutique. Her white cowboy hat had a long, filmy veil attached to the band. The flouncy, full skirt of her dress was perfect for dancing.

And they did dance. Starting with the first dance. Logan and Sarah held Sophia between them and swayed slowly to Keith Urban's "Making Memories of Us."

They served burgers for dinner and there was plenty of beer and soft drinks for all. Sarah's mom took Sophia home at a little after eight, where a nice girl from up the street was waiting to babysit so that Flo could return to the wedding celebration.

By eleven, a lot of the guests had gone home. But most of the younger men and women were still there when Sarah jumped up on the bar brandishing her wildflower bouquet. Lily caught it with a yelp of pure surprise.

"You're next!" Sarah called to her lifelong friend.

Lily laughed and shook her head. She didn't believe it. But Sarah just *knew*. If she could find the only man for her right here in her hometown, certainly Lily could do the same.

Logan was waiting when Sarah climbed down off the bar. He swept her into his arms and out onto the dance floor. They two-stepped through three numbers and then the music slowed. He pulled her nice and close.

"Why the Ace of all places?" he whispered in her ear.

"You love it."

"I do, yeah—but why did you choose it?"

She gazed up at him, golden-brown eyes gleaming, as they swayed to the music. "I guess because the Ace has always meant romance and possibility to me. I love it here. There's music, people talking and laughing. Everybody's having fun. Truthfully, I can't think of a more perfect setting for us to say 'I do.'"

Right then, Cole and Viv Dalton danced by. Viv and Sarah shared a smile. At the edge of the dance floor, Max was watching, looking way too pleased with himself.

Sarah smoothed the collar of Logan's white dress shirt. "Your dad is such a character. I mean, just look at him, grinning like that. What is he thinking?"

"You really don't know?"

"Not a clue."

Logan nuzzled her silky cheek. "He's thinking, *One down, five to go.*"

Sarah threw back her head and laughed as Logan pulled her closer. "What?" she demanded.

"This." And he claimed her lips in a slow, sweet kiss.

* * * * *

*Look for the next installment of the new continuity
Montana Mavericks: Six Brides for Six Brothers*

Don't miss
Rust Creek Falls Cinderella
by Melissa Senate

*On sale August 2019, wherever Harlequin books
and ebooks are sold.*

And look for Gemma and Hank's story,
The Maverick's Summer Sweetheart
*by Stacy Connelly,
available now!*

SPECIAL EXCERPT FROM

H HARLEQUIN®

SPECIAL EDITION

*To give the orphaned triplets they're guardians of the
stability they need, Lulu McCabe and Sam Kirkland
decide to jointly adopt them. But when it's discovered
their marriage wasn't actually annulled, they have
to prove to the courts they're responsible—
by renewing their vows!*

Read on for a sneak preview of Cathy Gillen Thacker's
Their Inherited Triplets,
the next book in the
Texas Legends: The McCabes miniseries.

"The two of you are still married," Liz said.

"Still?" Lulu croaked.

Sam asked, "What are you talking about?"

"More to the point, how do you know this?" Lulu
demanded, the news continuing to hit her like a gut punch.

Travis looked down at the papers in front of him.
"Official state records show you eloped in the Double
Knot Wedding Chapel in Memphis, Tennessee, on
Monday, March 14, nearly ten years ago. Alongside
another couple, Peter and Theresa Thompson, in a double
wedding ceremony."

Lulu gulped. "But our union was never legal," she
pointed out, trying to stay calm, while Sam sat beside her
in stoic silence.

Liz countered, "Ah, actually, it is legal. In fact, it's still
valid to this day."

Sam reached over and took her hand in his, much as he had the first time they had been in this room together. "How is that possible?" Lulu asked weakly.

"We never mailed in the certificate of marriage, along with the license, to the state of Tennessee," Sam said.

"And for our union to be recorded and therefore legal, we had to have done that," Lulu reiterated.

"Well, apparently, the owners of the Double Knot Wedding Chapel did, and your marriage was recorded. And is still valid to this day, near as we can tell. Unless you two got a divorce or an annulment somewhere else? Say another country?" Travis prodded.

"Why would we do that? We didn't know we were married," Sam returned.

Don't miss
Their Inherited Triplets *by Cathy Gillen Thacker,*
available August 2019 wherever
Harlequin® Special Edition books and ebooks are sold.

www.Harlequin.com

HSEEXP0719

SPECIAL EXCERPT FROM

H
HQN™

*Read on for a sneak peek at
the first funny and heart-tugging book in Jo McNally's
Rendezvous Falls series,* Slow Dancing at Sunrise*!*

"I'd have thought the idea of me getting caught in a rainstorm would make your day."

He gave her a quick glance. Just because she was off-limits didn't mean he was blind.

"Trust me, it did." Luke slowed the truck and reached behind the seat to grab his zippered hoodie hanging there. Whitney looked down and her cheeks flamed when she realized how her clothes were clinging to her. She snatched the hoodie from his hand before he could give it to her, and thrust her arms into it without offering any thanks. Even the zipper sounded pissed off when she yanked it closed.

"Perfect. Another guy with more testosterone than manners. Nice to know it's not just a Chicago thing. Jackasses are everywhere."

Luke frowned. He'd been having fun at her expense, figuring she'd give it right back to him as she had before. But her words hinted at a story that didn't reflect well on men in general. She'd been hurt. He shouldn't care. But that quick dimming of the fight in her eyes made him feel ashamed. *That* was a new experience.

A flash of lightning made her flinch. But the thunder didn't follow as quickly as the last time. The storm was moving off. He drove from the vineyard into the parking lot and over to the main house. The sound of the rain on the roof was less angry. But Whitney wasn't. She was clutching his sweatshirt around herself, her knuckles white. From anger? Embarrassment? Both? Luke shook his head.

"Look, I thought I was doing the right thing, driving up there." He rubbed the back of his neck and grimaced, remembering how sweaty and filthy he still was. "It's not my fault you walked out of the woods soaking wet. I mean, I try not to be a jackass, but I'm still a man. And I *did* offer my hoodie."

Whitney's chin pointed up toward the second floor of the main house. Her neck was long and graceful. There was a vein pulsing at the base of it. She blinked a few times, and for a horrifying moment, he thought there might be tears shimmering there in her eyes. *Damn it.* The last thing he needed was to have Helen's niece *crying* in his truck. He opened his mouth to say something—anything—but she beat him to it.

"I'll concede I wasn't prepared for rain." Her mouth barely moved, her words forced through clenched teeth. "But a gentleman would have looked away or…something."

His low laughter was enough to crack that brittle shell of hers. She turned to face him, eyes wide.

"See, Whitney, that's where you made your biggest mistake." He shrugged. "It wasn't going out for a day hike with a storm coming." He talked over her attempted objection. "Your *biggest* mistake was thinking I'm any kind of gentleman."

The corner of her mouth tipped up into an almost smile. "But you said you weren't a jackass."

"There's a hell of a lot of real estate between jackass and gentleman, babe."

Her half smile faltered, then returned. That familiar spark appeared in her eyes. The crack in her veneer had been repaired, and the sharp edge returned to her voice. Any other guy might have been annoyed, but Luke was oddly relieved to see Whitney back in fighting form.

"The fact that you just referred to me as 'babe' tells me you're a lot closer to jackass than you think."

He lifted his shoulder. "I never told you which end of the spectrum I fell on."

The rain had slowed to a steady drizzle. She reached for the door handle, looking over her shoulder with a smirk.

"Actually, I'm pretty sure you just did."

She hurried up the steps to the covered porch. He waited, but she didn't look back before going into the house. Her energy still filled the cab of the truck, and so did her scent. Spicy, woodsy, rain soaked. Finally coming to his senses, he threw the truck into Reverse and headed back toward the carriage house. He needed a long shower. A long *cold* one.

Don't miss
Jo McNally's Slow Dancing at Sunrise,
available July 2019 from HQN Books!

www.Harlequin.com